YORKSHIRE

A Literary Landscape

More regional anthologies
from Macmillan Collector's Library

Treasures of Cornwall: A Literary Anthology
edited by Luke Thompson

YORKSHIRE

A Literary Landscape

Edited and introduced by
DAVID STUART DAVIES

MACMILLAN COLLECTOR'S LIBRARY

This collection first published 2023 by Macmillan Collector's Library
an imprint of Pan Macmillan
The Smithson, 6 Briset Street, London EC1M 5NR
EU representative: Macmillan Publishers Ireland Ltd,
1st Floor, The Liffey Trust Centre, 117–126 Sheriff Street Upper,
Dublin 1, D01 YC43
Associated companies throughout the world
www.panmacmillan.com

ISBN 978-1-5290-9041-3

Selection, introduction and author biographies © David Stuart Davies 2023
Map of Yorkshire © Antiqua Print Gallery / Alamy Stock Photo

The permissions acknowledgements on p. 215 constitute an extension of
this copyright page.

3 5 7 9 8 6 4 2

A CIP catalogue record for this book is available from the British Library.

Typeset in Plantin by Jouve (UK), Milton Keynes
Printed and bound by TJ Books Ltd, Padstow, Cornwall PL28 8RW

Visit **www.panmacmillan.com** to read more
about all our books and to buy them.

Contents

TOWNS AND CITIES

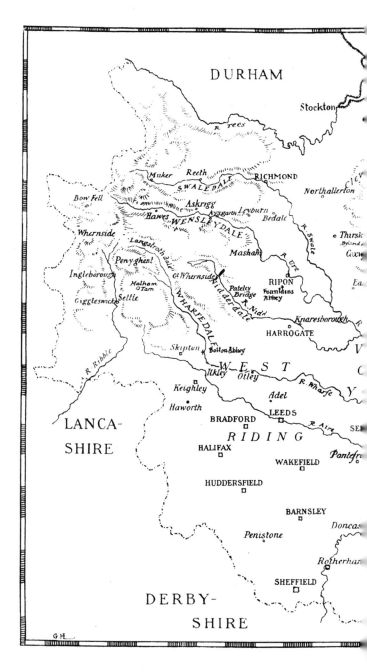

A Sketch Map of Yorkshire

Redcar
Saltburn
Staithes
Runswick
Danby Beacon
Sandsend
WHITBY
Eglon
Robin Hoods Bay
Goathland
Ravenscar
MOORS
Kirby Moorside
Pickering
VALE OF PICKERING
Cloughton
SCARBOROUGH
NORTH
Slingsby
R. Derwent
MALTON
FILEY
Cliffs
N. Grimstone
Wharram le Street
Rudstone
Flamborough Head
Castle Howard
Kirkham Abbey
Cowlam
Sledmere
Burton Agnes
BRIDLINGTON
Sheriff Hutton
Gt DRIFFIELD
SEA
Stamford Bridge
THE WOLDS
Skipsea
York
R. Derwent
Warter
Pocklington
HOLDERNESS
HORNSEA
Market Weighton
BEVERLEY
Hemingbrough
Wressle
Howden
Brough
HULL
Hedon
Withernsea
GOOLE
River
Humber
Patrington
Kilnsea
Isle of Ravenspur
Don
Spurn Head
LINCOLN-
SHIRE
R. Trent

SCALE OF MILES
5   10   15   20

On Ilkla Moor baht 'at

Wheear 'ast tha bin sin' ah saw thee, ah saw thee?
On Ilkla Mooar baht 'at
Wheear 'ast tha bin sin' ah saw thee, ah saw thee?
Wheear 'ast tha bin sin' ah saw thee?
On Ilkla Mooar baht 'at
On Ilkla Mooar baht 'at
On Ilkla Mooar baht 'at
Tha's been a cooartin' Mary Jane
Tha's bahn' to catch thy deeath o' cowd
Then us'll ha' to bury thee
Then t'worms'll come an' eyt thee up
Then t'ducks'll come an' eyt up t'worms
Then us'll go an' eyt up t'ducks
Then us'll all ha' etten thee
That's wheear we get us ooan back

Introduction

David Stuart Davies

For those who think of Yorkshire as the county where folk wander around wearing flat caps or even venture on to Ilkley Moor baht 'at, this book will come as a revelation. Allow me to tell you that Yorkshire, God's Own Country, as the natives think of it, is not only a county of lush pastures, beautiful undulating dales, starkly atmospheric moorland, picturesque seaside vistas, sturdy industrial towns and picture-book country cottages, but it has been the birthplace or the muse of many great artists, whether they be writers, painters, actors, performers, sculptors – the whole creative range of individuals who have enriched and continue to enrich our culture. In this book, we are concentrating on the wordsmiths who through prose and poetry have captured the essence of Yorkshire-ness in characters and scenery.

Returning to the poem 'On Ilkla Moor baht 'at', it is this well-known popular verse which is regarded as epitomizing the Yorkshire character, which at first glance appears to be dour and grumpy. However, on closer inspection of the lyrics one can observe a witty undercurrent of ironic humour woven into these lines, suggesting a lively wink and nod of knowing self-deprecating cheekiness. So it is with the native-born

Tykes, as will become apparent as you sample some of the lighter extracts in this collection.

There is also a rich history to be explored in the county. One only has to visit the cobbled streets of Haworth, home of the Brontës, or stand beneath the mellowed walls of the majestic York Minster, or climb up the 199 steps to Whitby Abbey to be transported into realms imbued with life of a bygone age, which continue to inspire a diverse range of writers.

As the county and its people are rich in contrasts, so was the aim of this book, to capture the diversity of landscape and people over the years. To do this, we have gathered the help of many great writers to weave their magic. Some, while not being born in Yorkshire, have for various reasons felt inspired to write about it; authors like Charles Dickens, Bram Stoker and Arthur Conan Doyle. However, the majority of contributions come from the pens of Yorkshire natives reaching back in time to such scribes as Cædmon and Andrew Marvell, on to the brilliant Brontë family and flavours of post-war angst from the likes of John Braine and Keith Waterhouse. Contemporary viewpoints are provided as well, namely from Ian McMillan – the Bard of Barnsley – and Amanda Owen, the Yorkshire shepherdess. There are pieces by Alan Bennett and Poet Laureate Simon Armitage too, both national treasures of high literary standing who are adept at illustrating the character of the county and the county's characters. So here, then, you have a wonderful patchwork that brings you a richly realized literary landscape.

In putting this collection together, one thought struck me with some ironical force. While all the pieces you will find in these pages focus on various aspects of Yorkshire and its people, there is at their heart a universality. There is nothing truly parochial about them. They speak to us all wherever we are in the world. I do believe they will speak to you, engage, entertain and, indeed, enlighten you. Enjoy.

YORKSHIRE

A Literary Landscape

COAST AND
COUNTRYSIDE

EMILY BRONTË
(1818–1848)

The Brontës are Britain's most remarkable family of authors, their work and lives linked closely to the brooding moorland of Haworth and Yorkshire. Most people know of Charlotte Brontë's novel *Jane Eyre* and Emily's *Wuthering Heights*, but their sister Anne wrote the groundbreaking early feminist novel *The Tenant of Wildfell Hall*, and their brother Branwell and father, the Reverend Patrick Brontë, were also published authors. A strong thread of elemental landscape and passion for nature runs through all their writings and, combined with a flair for the dramatic and the unflinching portrayal of some of the worst aspects of humanity, the Brontës exploded on to the mid-nineteenth-century literary world.

First published under the pseudonyms of Currer, Ellis and Acton Bell, names which were neither male nor female, the three sisters' 1846 collection of poems made little impact, but *Jane Eyre*, *Wuthering Heights* and *Agnes Grey*, all published in 1847, created a huge stir. Critics were impressed by the power of their work but also shocked by what they saw as 'coarse' and 'brutal' elements. Speculation around the Bells' identity added to the mystery. After Emily and Anne's early deaths, visitors began to flock to Haworth while Charlotte and her father were still alive, and fascination with the romantic myth of the tragic family of writers grew further with the publication of Elizabeth Gaskell's *The Life of Charlotte Brontë* in 1857.

Their home in Haworth, now the internationally famous Brontë Parsonage Museum, overlooking the overcrowded churchyard and perched on the edge of bleak and glorious Pennine moorland, was the creative heart of their lives. Two centuries on, anyone drawn to visit the area by the power of the Brontës' writing can still experience the wuthering Yorkshire landscape which inspired them.

High Waving Heather

High waving heather, 'neath stormy blasts bending,
Midnight and moonlight and bright shining stars;
Darkness and glory rejoicingly blending,
Earth rising to heaven and heaven descending,
Man's spirit away from its drear dongeon sending,
Bursting the fetters and breaking the bars.

All down the mountain sides, wild forest lending
One mighty voice to the life-giving wind;
Rivers their banks in the jubilee rending,
Fast through the valleys a reckless course wending,
Wider and deeper their waters extending,
Leaving a desolate desert behind.

Shining and lowering and swelling and dying,
Changing for ever from midnight to noon;
Roaring like thunder, like soft music sighing,
Shadows on shadows advancing and flying,
Lightning-bright flashes the deep gloom defying,
Coming as swiftly and fading as soon.

JAMES HERRIOT
(1916–1995)

James Herriot was the pen name of James Alfred Wight, who found fame by writing a series of books which gave a slightly fictionalized version of his experiences as a country vet in Yorkshire. Not only did he capture the pleasures and pains of his profession but provided evocative images of the Yorkshire Dales as a backdrop to his stories. He also had the knack of providing splendid details of the various colourful characters that he encountered on his rounds as the local vet. And one must not forget the humour, which is one of the mainstays of his fiction. In the 1970s, a television series based on the books, *All Creatures Great and Small*, increased their popularity, elevating Herriot to national treasure status. There is now a James Herriot Museum in the premises of his old surgery in Thirsk – the Darrowby of the books. In this extract, James Herriot helps deliver a calf and encounters Yorkshire farmers for the first time.

from All Creatures Great and Small

They didn't say anything about this in the books, I thought, as the snow blew in through the gaping doorway and settled on my naked back.

I lay face down on the cobbled floor in a pool of nameless muck, my arm deep inside the straining cow, my feet scrabbling for a toe hold between the stones. I was stripped to the waist and the snow mingled with the dirt and the dried blood on my body. I could see nothing outside the circle of flickering light thrown by the smoky oil lamp which the farmer held over me.

No, there wasn't a word in the books about searching for your ropes and instruments in the shadows; about trying to keep clean in a half bucket of tepid water; about the cobbles digging into your chest. Nor about the slow numbing of the arms, the creeping paralysis of the muscles as the fingers tried to work against the cow's powerful expulsive efforts.

There was no mention anywhere of the gradual exhaustion, the feeling of futility and the little far-off voice of panic.

My mind went back to that picture in the obstetrics book. A cow standing in the middle of a gleaming floor while a sleek veterinary surgeon in a spotless parturition overall inserted his arm to a polite distance. He was relaxed and smiling, the farmer and his helpers were smiling, even the cow was smiling. There was no dirt or blood or sweat anywhere.

That man in the picture had just finished an excellent lunch and had moved next door to do a bit of calving just for the sheer pleasure of it, as a kind of dessert. He hadn't crawled shivering from his bed at two o'clock in the morning and bumped over twelve miles of frozen snow, staring sleepily ahead till the lonely farm showed in the headlights. He hadn't climbed half a mile of white fell-side to the doorless barn where his patient lay.

I tried to wriggle my way an extra inch inside the cow. The calf's head was back and I was painfully pushing a thin, looped rope towards its lower jaw with my finger tips. All the time my arm was being squeezed between the calf and the bony pelvis. With every straining effort from the cow the pressure became almost unbearable, then she would relax and I would push the rope another inch. I wondered how long I would be able to keep this up. If I didn't snare that jaw soon I would never get the calf away. I groaned, set my teeth and reached forward again.

Another little flurry of snow blew in and I could almost hear the flakes sizzling on my sweating back. There was sweat on my forehead too, and it trickled into my eyes as I pushed.

There is always a time at a bad calving when you begin to wonder if you will ever win the battle. I had reached this stage.

Little speeches began to flit through my brain. 'Perhaps it would be better to slaughter this cow. Her pelvis is so small and narrow that I can't see a calf coming through,' or 'She's a good fat animal and really of the beef type, so don't you think it would pay you better to get the butcher?' or perhaps 'This is a very bad presentation. In a roomy cow it would be simple enough to bring the head round but in this case it is just about impossible.'

Of course, I could have delivered the calf by embryotomy – by passing a wire over the neck and sawing off the head. So many of these occasions ended with the floor strewn with heads, legs, heaps of intestines. There were thick textbooks devoted to the countless ways you could cut up a calf.

But none of it was any good here, because this calf was alive. At my furthest stretch I had got my finger as far as the commissure of the mouth and had been startled by a twitch of the little creature's tongue. It was unexpected because calves in this position are usually dead, asphyxiated by the acute flexion of the neck and the pressure of the dam's powerful contractions. But this one had a spark of life in it and if it came out it would have to be in one piece.

I went over to my bucket of water, cold now and bloody, and silently soaped my arms. Then I lay down again, feeling the cobbles harder than ever against my chest. I worked my toes between the stones, shook the sweat from my eyes and for the hundredth time thrust an arm that felt like spaghetti into the cow; alongside the little dry legs of the calf, like sandpaper tearing against my flesh, then to the bend in the neck and so to the ear and then, agonisingly, along the side of the face towards the lower jaw which had become my major goal in life.

It was incredible that I had been doing this for nearly two hours; fighting as my strength ebbed to push a little noose round that jaw. I had tried everything else – repelling a leg, gentle traction with a blunt hook in the eye socket, but I was back to the noose.

It had been a miserable session all through. The farmer, Mr Dinsdale, was a long, sad, silent man of few words who always seemed to be expecting the worst to happen. He had a long, sad, silent son with him and the two of them had watched my efforts with deepening gloom.

But worst of all had been Uncle. When I had first entered the hillside barn I had been surprised to see a little bright-eyed old man in a pork pie hat settling down comfortably on a bale of straw. He was filling his pipe and clearly looking forward to the entertainment.

'Now then, young man,' he cried in the nasal twang of the West Riding. 'I'm Mr Dinsdale's brother. I farm over in Listondale.'

I put down my equipment and nodded. 'How do you do? My name is Herriot.'

The old man looked me over, piercingly. 'My vet is Mr Broomfield. Expect you'll have heard of him – everybody knows him, I reckon. Wonderful man, Mr Broomfield, especially at calving. Do you know, I've never seen 'im beat yet.'

I managed a wan smile. Any other time I would have been delighted to hear how good my colleague was, but somehow not now, not now. In fact, the words set a mournful little bell tolling inside me.

'No, I'm afraid I don't know Mr Broomfield,' I said, taking off my jacket and, more reluctantly, peeling my shirt over my head. 'But I haven't been around these parts very long.'

Uncle was aghast. 'You don't know him! Well you're the only one as doesn't. They think the world of him in Listondale, I can tell you.' He lapsed into a shocked silence and applied a match to his pipe. Then he shot a glance at my goose-pimpled torso. 'Strips like a boxer does Mr Broomfield. Never seen such muscles on a man.'

A wave of weakness coursed sluggishly over me. I felt suddenly leaden-footed and inadequate. As I began to lay out my ropes and instruments on a clean towel the old man spoke again.

'And how long have you been qualified, may I ask?'

'Oh, about seven months.'

'Seven months!' Uncle smiled indulgently, tamped down his tobacco and blew out a cloud of rank, blue smoke. 'Well, there's nowt like a bit of experience, I always says. Mr Broomfield's been doing my work now for over ten years and he really knows what he's about. No, you can 'ave your book learning. Give me experience every time.'

I tipped some antiseptic into the bucket and lathered my arms carefully. I knelt behind the cow.

'Mr Broomfield always puts some special lubricating oils on his arms first,' Uncle said, pulling contentedly on his pipe. 'He says you get infection of the womb if you just use soap and water.'

I made my first exploration. It was the burdened

moment all vets go through when they first put their hand into a cow. Within seconds I would know whether I would be putting on my jacket in fifteen minutes or whether I had hours of hard labour ahead of me.

I was going to be unlucky this time; it was a nasty presentation. Head back and no room at all; more like being inside an undeveloped heifer than a second calver. And she was bone dry – the 'waters' must have come away from her hours ago. She had been running out on the high fields and had started to calve a week before her time; that was why they had had to bring her into this half-ruined barn. Anyway, it would be a long time before I saw my bed again.

'Well now, what have you found, young man?' Uncle's penetrating voice cut through the silence. 'Head back, eh? You won't have much trouble, then. I've seen Mr Broomfield do 'em like that – he turns calf right round and brings it out back legs first.'

I had heard this sort of nonsense before. A short time in practice had taught me that all farmers were experts with other farmers' livestock. When their own animals were in trouble they tended to rush to the phone for the vet, but with their neighbours' they were confident, knowledgeable and full of helpful advice. And another phenomenon I had observed was that their advice was usually regarded as more valuable than the vet's. Like now, for instance; Uncle was obviously an accepted sage and the Dinsdales listened with deference to everything he said.

'Another way with a job like this,' continued Uncle,

'is to get a few strong chaps with ropes and pull the thing out, head back and all.'

I gasped as I felt my way around. 'I'm afraid it's impossible to turn a calf completely round in this small space. And to pull it out without bringing the head round would certainly break the mother's pelvis.'

The Dinsdales narrowed their eyes. Clearly they thought I was hedging in the face of Uncle's superior knowledge.

And now, two hours later, defeat was just round the corner. I was just about whacked. I had rolled and grovelled on the filthy cobbles while the Dinsdales watched me in morose silence and Uncle kept up a non-stop stream of comment. Uncle, his ruddy face glowing with delight, his little eyes sparkling, hadn't had such a happy night for years. His long trek up the hillside had been repaid a hundredfold. His vitality was undiminished; he had enjoyed every minute.

As I lay there, eyes closed, face stiff with dirt, mouth hanging open, Uncle took his pipe in his hand and leaned forward on his straw bale. 'You're about beat, young man,' he said with deep satisfaction. 'Well, I've never seen Mr Broomfield beat but he's had a lot of experience. And what's more, he's strong, really strong. That's one man you couldn't tire.'

Rage flooded through me like a draught of strong spirit. The right thing to do, of course, would be to get up, tip the bucket of bloody water over Uncle's head, run down the hill and drive away; away from Yorkshire, from Uncle, from the Dinsdales, from this cow.

Instead, I clenched my teeth, braced my legs and pushed with everything I had; and with a sensation of disbelief I felt my noose slide over the sharp little incisor teeth and into the calf's mouth. Gingerly, muttering a prayer, I pulled on the thin rope with my left hand and felt the slipknot tighten. I had hold of that lower jaw.

At last I could start doing something. 'Now hold this rope, Mr Dinsdale, and just keep a gentle tension on it. I'm going to repel the calf and if you pull steadily at the same time, the head ought to come round.'

'What if the rope comes off?' asked Uncle hopefully.

I didn't answer. I put my hand in against the calf's shoulder and began to push against the cow's contractions. I felt the small body moving away from me. 'Now a steady pull, Mr Dinsdale, without jerking.' And to myself, 'Oh God, don't let it slip off.'

The head was coming round. I could feel the neck straightening against my arm, then the ear touched my elbow. I let go the shoulder and grabbed the little muzzle. Keeping the teeth away from the vaginal wall with my hand, I guided the head till it was resting where it should be, on the fore limbs.

Quickly I extended the noose till it reached behind the ears. 'Now pull on the head as she strains.'

'Nay, you should pull on the legs now,' cried Uncle.

'Pull on the bloody head rope, I tell you!' I bellowed at the top of my voice and felt immediately better as Uncle retired, offended, to his bale.

With traction the head was brought out and the rest of the body followed easily. The little animal lay motionless on the cobbles, eyes glassy and unseeing, tongue blue and grossly swollen.

'It'll be dead. Bound to be,' grunted Uncle, returning to the attack.

I cleared the mucus from the mouth, blew hard down the throat and began artificial respiration. After a few pressures on the ribs, the calf gave a gasp and the eyelids flickered. Then it started to inhale and one leg jerked.

Uncle took off his hat and scratched his head in disbelief. 'By gaw, it's alive. I'd have thowt it'd sure to be dead after you'd messed about all that time.' A lot of the fire had gone out of him and his pipe hung down empty from his lips.

'I know what this little fellow wants,' I said. I grasped the calf by its fore legs and pulled it up to its mother's head. The cow was stretched out on her side, her head extended wearily along the rough floor. Her ribs heaved, her eyes were almost closed; she looked past caring about anything. Then she felt the calf's body against her face and there was a transformation; her eyes opened wide and her muzzle began a snuffling exploration of the new object. Her interest grew with every sniff and she struggled on to her chest, nosing and probing all over the calf, rumbling deep in her chest. Then she began to lick him methodically. Nature provides the perfect stimulant massage for a time like this and the little creature arched his back as the coarse papillae on the tongue dragged along his skin. Within a minute he was shaking his head and trying to sit up.

I grinned. This was the bit I liked. The little miracle. I felt it was something that would never grow stale no matter how often I saw it. I cleaned as much of the dried blood and filth from my body as I could, but most of it had caked on my skin and not even my finger nails would move it. It would have to wait for the hot bath at home. Pulling my shirt over my head, I felt as though I had been beaten for a long time with a thick stick. Every muscle ached. My mouth was dried out, my lips almost sticking together.

A long, sad figure hovered near. 'How about a drink?' asked Mr Dinsdale.

I could feel my grimy face cracking into an incredulous smile. A vision of hot tea well laced with whisky swam before me. 'That's very kind of you, Mr Dinsdale, I'd love a drink. It's been a hard two hours.'

'Nay,' said Mr Dinsdale looking at me steadily, 'I meant for the cow.'

I began to babble. 'Oh yes, of course, certainly, by all means give her a drink. She must be very thirsty. It'll do her good. Certainly, certainly, give her a drink.'

I gathered up my tackle and stumbled out of the barn. On the moor it was still dark and a bitter wind whipped over the snow, stinging my eyes. As I plodded down the slope, Uncle's voice, strident and undefeated, reached me for the last time.

'Mr Broomfield doesn't believe in giving a drink after calving. Says it chills the stomach.'

DOROTHY UNA RADCLIFFE
(1887–1967)

Dorothy Una Ratcliffe was a remarkable woman and a
self-appointed Yorkshire lass, despite being born in
Sussex and educated in Surrey. Reference books refer
to her as a socialite, heiress and author. In the latter role
she published forty-nine books, many in the Yorkshire
dialect, which she studied in an academic way, allowing
her to capture the natural Yorkshire rhythm, vocabulary
and authentic flavour of the verse, as demonstrated by
the two poems in this book.

April in Wensleydale

Snow's powdering bare Addleborough,
And white are Penhill and Whernside;
Up on the high exposed moorlands
It seems as tho' April had lied;
For buds they are wee on the rowans,
Slow the unleafing of thorn,
But curlews call over the heather
And soon will the young ones be born.

At Hardraw, at Gayle, there are catkins,
At Aysgarth the hawthorn has buds,
At Bainbridge the blackthorn's in blossom
And windflowers troop in the woods;
And April is winning at Leyburn,
Her primroses storming the Shawl,
Cuckoo-pint, mercury, violets,
Celandines round Nappa Hall.

Tho' snow is still seen on the moorlands,
And winds are companioned by hail,
Yet April—the year's fortune-teller—
Is gypsying right up the dale.
Quiet she came to the dale-end,
Hand linked in hand with the showers,
But she'll leave in a medley of music,
She'll leave in a revel of flowers.

BRAM STOKER
(1847–1912)

Bram Stoker visited Whitby on holiday in 1882 and became so fascinated by the Yorkshire seaside town that he determined that it would feature significantly in the strange novel he was writing about the Transylvanian vampire Count Dracula. It was in Whitby that the Russian schooner *Demeter*, which is transporting Dracula, entombed in a coffin filled with his own native earth, foundered and was wrecked on the shore. The storm that drives the *Demeter* onto to rocks is some of Stoker's most elegant descriptive writing, capturing in vigorous style the drama of the scene.

from Dracula

Shortly before ten o'clock the stillness of the air grew quite oppressive, and the silence was so marked that the bleating of a sheep inland or the barking of a dog in the town was distinctly heard, and the band on the pier, with its lively French air, was like a discord in the great harmony of nature's silence. A little after midnight came a strange sound from over the sea, and high overhead the air began to carry a strange, faint hollow booming.

Then without warning the tempest broke. With a rapidity which, at the time, seemed incredible, and even afterwards is impossible to realise, the whole aspect of nature at once became convulsed. The waves rose in growing fury, each over-topping its fellow, till in a very few minutes the lately glassy sea was like a roaring and devouring monster. White-crested waves beat madly on the level sands and rushed up the shelving cliffs; others broke over the piers, and with their spume swept the lanthorns of the lighthouses which rise from the end of either pier of Whitby Harbour. The wind roared like thunder, and blew with such force that it was with difficulty that even strong men kept their feet, or clung with grim clasp to the iron stanchions. It was found necessary to clear the entire piers from the mass of onlookers, or else the fatalities of the night would have been increased manyfold. To add to the difficulties and dangers of the time, masses of sea-fog came drifting inland – white, wet clouds, which swept by in ghostly fashion, so dank and damp and cold that it needed but little effort of imagination to think that the spirits of those lost at sea were touching their living brethren with the clammy hands of death, and many a one shuddered as the wreaths of sea-mist swept by. At times the mist cleared, and the sea for some distance could be seen in the glare of the lightning, which now came thick and fast, followed by such sudden peals of thunder that the whole sky overhead seemed trembling under the shock of the footsteps of the storm. Some of the scenes thus revealed were of immeasurable grandeur and of absorbing interest – the sea, running mountains high, threw skywards with each wave mighty masses of white foam, which the tempest seemed to snatch at and whirl away into space; here and there a fishing-boat, with a rag of sail, running madly for shelter before the blast; now and again the white wings of a storm-tossed sea-bird. On the summit of the East Cliff the new searchlight was ready for experiment, but had not yet been tried. The officers in charge of it got it into working order, and in the pauses of the inrushing mist swept with it the surface of the sea. Once or twice its service was most effective, as when a fishing-boat, with gunwale under water, rushed into the harbour, able, by the guidance of the sheltering light, to avoid the danger of dashing against the piers. As each boat achieved the safety of the port there was a shout of joy from the mass of people on shore, a shout which for a moment seemed to cleave the gale and was then swept away in its rush. Before long the searchlight discovered some distance away a schooner with all sails set, apparently the same vessel which had been noticed earlier in the evening. The wind had by this time backed to the east, and there was a shudder amongst the watchers on the cliff as they realised the terrible danger in which she now was. Between her and the port lay the great flat reef on which so many good ships have from time to time suffered, and, with the wind blowing from its present quarter, it would be quite impossible that she should fetch the entrance of the harbour. It was now nearly the hour of high tide, but the waves were so great that in their troughs the shallows of the shore were almost visible, and the schooner, with all sails set, was rushing with such speed that, in the words of one old salt, 'she must fetch up somewhere, if it was only in hell.' Then came another rush of sea-fog, greater than any hitherto – a mass of dank mist, which seemed to close on all things like a grey pall, and left available to men only the organ of hearing, for the roar of the tempest, and the crash of the thunder, and the booming of the mighty billows came through the damp oblivion even louder than before. The rays of the searchlight were kept fixed on the harbour mouth across the East Pier, where the shock was expected, and men waited breathless. The wind suddenly shifted to the north-east, and the remnant of the sea-fog melted in the blast; and then, *mirabile dictu*, between the piers, leaping from wave to wave as it rushed at headlong speed, swept the strange schooner before the blast, with all sails set, and gained the safety of the harbour. The searchlight followed her, and a shudder ran through all who saw her, for lashed to the helm was a corpse, with drooping head, which swung horribly to and fro at each motion of the ship. No other form could be seen on deck at all. A great awe came on all as they realised that the ship, as if by a miracle, had found the harbour, unsteered save by the hand of a dead man! However, all took place more quickly than it takes to write these words. The schooner paused not, but rushing across the harbour, pitched herself on that accumulation of sand and gravel washed by many tides and many storms into the south-east corner of the pier jutting under the East Cliff, known locally as Tate Hill Pier.

There was of course a considerable concussion as the vessel drove up on the sand-heap. Every spar, rope, and stay was strained, and some of the 'top-hamper' came crashing down. But, strangest of all, the very instant the shore was touched, an immense dog sprang up on deck from below, as if shot up by the concussion, and running forward, jumped from the bow on to the sand. Making straight for the steep cliff, where the churchyard hangs over the laneway to the East Pier so steeply that some of the flat tombstones – 'thruff-steans' or 'through-stones', as they call them in the Whitby vernacular – actually project over where the sustaining cliff has fallen away, it disappeared in the darkness, which seemed intensified just beyond the focus of the searchlight.

It so happened that there was no one at the moment on Tate Hill Pier, as all those whose houses are in close proximity were either in bed or were out on the heights above. Thus the coastguard on duty on the eastern side of the harbour, who at once ran down to the little pier, was the first to climb on board. The men working the searchlight, after scouring the entrance of the harbour without seeing anything, then turned the light on the derelict and kept it there. The coastguard ran aft, and when he came beside the wheel, bent over to examine it and recoiled at once as though under some sudden emotion. This seemed to pique the general curiosity, and quite a number of people began to run. It is a good way round from the West Cliff by the Drawbridge to Tate Hill Pier, but your correspondent is a fairly good runner, and came well ahead of the crowd. When I arrived, however, I found already assembled on the pier a crowd, whom the coastguard and police refused to allow to come on board. By the courtesy of the chief boatman, I was, as your correspondent, permitted to climb on deck, and was one of a small group who saw that dead seaman whilst actually lashed to the wheel.

It was no wonder that the coastguard was surprised, or even awed, for not often can such a sight have been seen. The man was simply fastened by his hands, tied one over the other, to a spoke of the wheel. Between the inner hand and the wood was a crucifix, the set of beads on which it was fastened being around both wrists and wheel, and all kept fast by the binding cords. The poor fellow may have been seated at one time, but the flapping and buffeting of the sails had worked through the rudder of the wheel and dragged him to and fro, so that the cords with which he was tied had cut the flesh to the bone. Accurate note was made of the state of things, and a doctor – Surgeon J. M. Caffyn, of 33, East Elliot Place – who came immediately after me, declared, after making examination, that the man must have been dead for quite two days. In his pocket was a bottle, carefully corked, empty save for a little roll of paper, which proved to be the addendum to the log. The coastguard said the man must have tied up his own hands, fastening the knots with his teeth. The fact that a coastguard was the first on board may save some complications, later on, in the Admiralty Court; for the coastguards cannot claim the salvage which is the right of the first civilian entering on a derelict. Already, however, the legal tongues are wagging, and one young law student is loudly asserting that the rights of the owner are already completely sacrificed, his property being held in contravention of the statutes of mortmain, since the tiller, as emblemship, if not proof, of delegated possession, is held in a *dead hand*. It is needless to say that the dead steersman has been reverently removed from the place where he held his honourable watch and ward till death – a steadfastness as noble as that of the young Casabianca – and placed in the mortuary to await inquest.

Already the sudden storm is passing, and its fierceness is abating; the crowds are scattering homewards, and the sky is beginning to redden over the Yorkshire wolds. I shall send, in time for your next issue, further details of the derelict ship which found her way so miraculously into harbour in the storm.

TED HUGHES
(1930–1998)

Ted Hughes was born in the little town of Mytholmroyd in West Yorkshire in 1930 and grew up to be one of the most talented poets of his generation. He was appointed Poet Laureate in 1984 and held the office until his death in 1988. The brilliance of his poetry often deals with the innocent savagery of animals or the wild untamed ferocity of nature. Animals serve as a metaphor for Hughes's view on life, relating their struggle for survival to the way that humans strive for ascendancy and survival. This theme is epitomized in the poem 'Pike', in which the poet is both repulsed and fascinated by this 'submarine of delicacy and horror'. He describes the creature with accuracy; his Yorkshire voice is inherent in the terse, economical yet powerful phrasing.

Pike

Pike, three inches long, perfect
Pike in all parts, green tigering the gold.
Killers from the egg: the malevolent aged grin.
They dance on the surface among the flies.

Or move, stunned by their own grandeur
Over a bed of emerald, silhouette
Of submarine delicacy and horror.
A hundred feet long in their world.

In ponds, under the heat-struck lily pads—
Gloom of their stillness:
Logged on last year's black leaves, watching upwards.
Or hung in an amber cavern of weeds

The jaws' hooked clamp and fangs
Not to be changed at this date;
A life subdued to its instrument;
The gills kneading quietly, and the pectorals.

Three we kept behind glass,
Jungled in weed: three inches, four,
And four and a half: fed fry to them—
Suddenly there were two. Finally one.

With a sag belly and the grin it was born with.
And indeed they spare nobody.
Two, six pounds each, over two feet long,
High and dry and dead in the willow-herb—

One jammed past its gills down the other's gullet:
The outside eye stared: as a vice locks—
The same iron in this eye
Though its film shrank in death.

A pond I fished, fifty yards across,
Whose lilies and muscular tench
Had outlasted every visible stone
Of the monastery that planted them—

Stilled legendary depth:
It was as deep as England. It held
Pike too immense to stir, so immense and old
That past nightfall I dared not cast

But silently cast and fished
With the hair frozen on my head
For what might move, for what eye might move.
The still splashes on the dark pond,

Owls hushing the floating woods
Frail on my ear against the dream
Darkness beneath night's darkness had freed,
That rose slowly towards me, watching.

PATRICK BRONTË
(1777–1861)

The Brontës' father, the Reverend Patrick Brontë, moved from poor beginnings in rural Ireland to a scholarship at Cambridge University before entering the church. After being widowed in 1821 and losing his two eldest daughters, Maria and Elizabeth, as children just a few years later, Patrick became the major influence on his remaining family, supporting their love of literature and ensuring that his daughters had access to a wide range of learning, something which was not common for women in nineteenth-century England. The Brontës were not wealthy, and he expected that his children would need to earn a living. This sermon preached at Haworth Church in 1824 tells of his worry when his young children went for a walk, and how he feared them lost in a dramatic storm on the moors.

A Sermon *from* A Man of Sorrow: The Life, Letters, and Times of the Rev. Patrick Brontë, 1777–1861

As the day was exceedingly fine, I had sent my little children, who were indisposed, accompanied by the servants, to take an airing on the common, and as they stayed rather longer than I expected, I went to an upper chamber to look out for their return. The heavens over the moors were blackening fast. I heard mutterings of distant thunder, and saw the frequent flashing of the lightning. Though, ten minutes before, there was scarcely a breath of air stirring; the gale freshened rapidly, and carried along with it clouds of dust and stubble; and, by this time, some large drops of rain, clearly announced an approaching heavy shower. My little family had escaped to a place of shelter, but I did not know it. I consequently watched every movement of the coming tempest with a painful degree of interest.

DANIEL DEFOE
(c. 1660–1731)

'I was born in the year 1632, in the city of York, of a
good family though not of that country, my father being
a foreigner who settled first at Hull . . .'

Thus begins the story of *Robinson Crusoe*, loosely based
on Alexander Selkirk, a Scottish sailor abandoned in
1704 on Más a Tierra in the Juan Fernández Islands at
his own request after a dispute with the ship's captain.
The author of this classic tale, published in 1719, was
Daniel Defoe. Born Daniel Foe, son of a London
butcher, he later added 'De', believing it sounded aris-
tocratic. He is best remembered for his novel *Robinson
Crusoe*, part of which was written in the Yorkshire
town of Halifax when he was staying at the Rose and
Crown Inn.

Although Crusoe's desert island is many miles away
from Halifax, it seems appropriate to present an extract
from the book which was partly penned in a Yorkshire
hostelry.

from Robinson Crusoe

June 18. Rained all day, and I stayed within. I thought at this time the rain felt cold, and I was something chilly, which I knew was not usual in that latitude.

June 19. Very ill, and shivering, as if the weather had been cold.

June 20. No rest all night; violent pains in my head, and feverish.

June 21. Very ill, frighted almost to death with the apprehensions of my sad condition, to be sick and no help. Prayed to God for the first time since the storm off of Hull, but scarce knew what I said, or why; my thoughts being all confused.

June 22. A little better, but under dreadful apprehensions of sickness.

June 23. Very bad again, cold and shivering, and then a violent headache.

June 24. Much better.

June 25. An ague very violent; the fit held me seven hours, cold fit and hot, with faint sweats after it.

June 26. Better; and having no victuals to eat, took my gun, but found myself very weak; however, I killed a she-goat and with much difficulty got it home and broiled some of it and ate; I would fain have stewed it and made some broth, but had no pot.

June 27. The ague again so violent that I lay abed all day and neither ate nor drank. I was ready to perish for thirst, but so weak I had not strength to stand up or to get myself any water to drink. Prayed to God again, but was lightheaded; and when I was not, I was so ignorant that I knew not what to say; only I lay and cried, "Lord look upon me! Lord pity me! Lord have mercy upon me!" I suppose I did nothing else for two or three hours till, the fit wearing off, I fell asleep, and did not wake till far in the night; when I waked, I found myself much refreshed, but weak, and exceeding thirsty. However, as I had no water in my whole habitation, I was forced to lie till morning and went to sleep again. In this second sleep I had this terrible dream.

I thought that I was sitting on the ground, on the outside of my wall, where I sat when the storm blew after the earthquake, and that I saw a man descend from a great black cloud, in a bright flame of fire, and light upon the ground. He was all over as bright as a flame, so that I could but just bear to look towards him; his countenance was most inexpressibly dreadful, impossible for words to describe; when he stepped upon the ground with his feet, I thought the earth trembled, just as it had done before in the earthquake, and all the air looked, to my apprehension, as if it had been filled with flashes of fire.

He was no sooner landed upon the earth but he moved forward towards me, with a long spear or weapon in his hand, to kill me; and when he came to a rising ground, at some distance, he spoke to me, or I heard a voice so terrible, that it is impossible to express the terror of it; all that I can say I understood was this: "Seeing all these things have not brought thee to repentance, now thou shalt die." At which words, I thought he lifted up the spear that was in his hand to kill me.

No one that shall ever read this account will expect that I should be able to describe the horrors of my soul at this terrible vision; I mean, that even while it was a dream, I even dreamed of those horrors; nor is it any more possible to describe the impression that remained upon my mind when I awaked and found it was but a dream.

I had, alas! no divine knowledge; what I had received by the good instruction of my father was then worn out by an uninterrupted series, for eight years, of seafaring wickedness, and a constant conversation with nothing but such as were like myself, wicked and profane to the last degree. I do not remember that I had in all that time one thought that so much as tended either to looking upwards towards God or inwards towards a reflection upon my own ways. But a certain stupidity of soul, without desire of good, or conscience of evil, had entirely overwhelmed me, and I was all that the most hardened, unthinking, wicked creature among our common sailors can be supposed to be, not having the least sense, either of the fear of God in danger or of thankfulness to God in deliverances.

In the relating what is already past of my story, this will be the more easily believed, when I shall add, that through all the variety of miseries that had to this day befallen me, I never had so much as one thought of it being the hand of God, or that it was a just punishment for my sin, my rebellious behaviour against my father, or my present sins, which were great; or so much as a punishment for the general course of my wicked life. When I was on the desperate expedition on the desert shores of Africa, I never had so much as one thought of what would become of me; or one wish to God to direct me whither I should go, or to keep me from the danger which apparently surrounded me, as well from voracious creatures as cruel savages. But I was merely thoughtless of a God, or a Providence, acted like a mere brute from the principles of nature, and by the dictates of common sense only, and indeed hardly that.

When I was delivered and taken up at sea by the Portugal captain, well used, and dealt justly and honourably with, as well as charitably, I had not the least thankfulness in my thoughts. When again I was shipwrecked, ruined, and in danger of drowning on this island, I was as far from remorse or looking on it as a judgment; I only said to myself often that I was an unfortunate dog and born to be always miserable.

It is true, when I got on shore first here, and found all my ship's crew drowned and myself spared, I was surprised with a kind of ecstasy, and some transports of soul which, had the grace of God assisted, might have come up to true thankfulness; but it ended where it began, in a mere common flight of joy, or, as I may say, *being glad I was alive*, without the least reflection upon the distinguishing goodness of the hand which had preserved me, and had singled me out to be preserved, when all the rest were destroyed; or an inquiry why Providence had been thus merciful to me; even just the same common sort of joy which seamen generally have after they are got safe ashore from a shipwreck, which they drown all in the next bowl of punch and forget almost as soon as it is over, and all the rest of my life was like it.

Even when I was afterwards, on due consideration, made sensible of my condition, how I was cast on this dreadful place, out of the reach of human kind, out of all hope of relief, or prospect of redemption, as soon as I saw but a prospect of living and that I should not starve and perish for hunger, all the sense of my affliction wore off, and I began to be very easy, applied myself to the works proper for my preservation and supply, and was far enough from being afflicted at my condition, as a judgment from Heaven, or as the hand of God against me; these were thoughts which very seldom entered into my head.

ANDREW MARVELL
(1621–1678)

Andrew Marvell was born in Winestead-in-Holderness, near the city of Kingston upon Hull. He was educated at Hull Grammar School and Trinity College, Cambridge. Marvell is regarded as one of the most notable metaphysical poets. He was also a politician and a satirist. In this beautiful poem, Marvell describes the pleasure of quiet contemplation in the green shade of a garden.

The Garden

How vainly men themselves amaze
To win the palm, the oak, or bays;
And their incessant labours see
Crowned from some single herb, or tree,
Whose short and narrow-vergèd shade
Does prudently their toils upbraid;
While all flow'rs and all trees do close
To weave the garlands of repose.

Fair Quiet, have I found thee here,
And Innocence, thy sister dear?
Mistaken long, I sought you then
In busy companies of men.
Your sacred plants, if here below,
Only among the plants will grow;
Society is all but rude
To this delicious solitude.

No white nor red was ever seen
So amorous as this lovely green.
Fond lovers, cruel as their flame,
Cut in these trees their mistress' name:
Little, alas! they know or heed
How far these beauties hers exceed!
Fair trees! wheres'e'er your barks I wound
No name shall but your own be found.

When we have run our passion's heat,
Love hither makes his best retreat.
The Gods, that mortal beauty chase,
Still in a tree did end their race;
Apollo hunted Daphne so,
Only that she might laurel grow;
And Pan did after Syrinx speed,
Not as a nymph, but for a reed.

What wondrous life is this I lead!
Ripe apples drop about my head;
The luscious clusters of the vine
Upon my mouth do crush their wine;
The nectarine, and curious peach,
Into my hands themselves do reach;
Stumbling on melons, as I pass,
Insnared with flowers, I fall on grass.

Meanwhile, the mind, from pleasure less,
Withdraws into its happiness:
The mind, that ocean where each kind
Does straight its own resemblance find;
Yet it creates, transcending these,
Far other worlds, and other seas;
Annihilating all that's made
To a green thought in a green shade.

Here at the fountain's sliding foot,
Or at some fruit-tree's mossy root,
Casting the body's vest aside,

My soul into the boughs does glide;
There like a bird it sits, and sings,
Then whets and claps its silver wings;
And, till prepared for longer flight,
Waves in its plumes the various light.

Such was that happy garden-state,
While man there walked without a mate:
After a place so pure and sweet,
What other help could yet be meet!
But 'twas beyond a mortal's share
To wander solitary there:
Two paradises 'twere in one,
To live in Paradise alone.

How well the skilful gardener drew
Of flowers, and herbs, this dial new;
Where, from above, the milder sun
Does through a fragrant zodiac run;
And, as it works, the industrious bee
Computes its time as well as we.
How could such sweet and wholesome hours
Be reckoned but with herbs and flowers!

FRANCES HODGSON BURNETT
(1849–1924)

Frances Hodgson Burnett's novel *The Secret Garden* is a children's classic featuring the young orphan Mary Lennox, a rather horrid and selfish young girl who is sent to stay with her uncle in Yorkshire. At first she hates her new home, the people living in it and, most of all, the bleak moors surrounding the house. However, her life changes dramatically when she finds her way into a secret garden on the estate. A robin leads her to discover the key to a hidden door which allows access to the secret plot. As she tends the plants, reinvigorating the soil, not only does the garden flourish but a magical process of regeneration of the family who live in the big house also takes place. The novel, first published in 1911, illustrates that if something is neglected it withers and dies, but when it is cared for it thrives. Here, Mary visits the garden for the first time.

from The Secret Garden

It was the sweetest, most mysterious-looking place anyone could imagine. The high walls which shut it in were covered with the leafless stems of climbing roses, which were so thick that they were matted together. Mary Lennox knew they were roses because she had seen a great many roses in India. All the ground was covered with grass of a wintry brown, and out of it grew clumps of bushes which were surely rose-bushes if they were alive. There were numbers of standard roses which had so spread their branches that they were like little trees. There were other trees in the garden, and one of the things which made the place look strangest and loveliest was that climbing roses had run all over them and swung down long tendrils which made light swaying curtains, and here and there they had caught at each other or at a far-reaching branch and had crept from one tree to another and made lovely bridges of themselves. There were neither leaves nor roses on them now, and Mary did not know whether they were dead or alive, but their thin grey or brown branches and sprays looked like a sort of hazy mantle spreading over everything, walls, and trees, and even brown grass, where they had fallen from their fastenings and run along the ground. It was this hazy tangle from tree to tree which made it all look so mysterious. Mary had thought it must be different from other gardens which had not been left all by themselves so long; and, indeed, it was different from any other place she had ever seen in her life.

'How still it is!' she whispered. 'How still!'

Then she waited a moment and listened at the stillness. The robin, who had flown to his tree-top, was still as all the rest. He did not even flutter his wings; he sat without stirring, and looked at Mary.

'No wonder it is still,' she whispered again. 'I am the first person who has spoken in here for ten years.'

She moved away from the door, stepping as softly as if she were afraid of awakening someone. She was glad that there was grass under her feet and that her steps made no sounds. She walked under one of the fairy-like grey arches between the trees and looked up at the sprays and tendrils which formed them.

'I wonder if they are all quite dead,' she said. 'Is it all a quite dead garden? I wish it wasn't.'

If she had been Ben Weatherstaff she could have told whether the wood was alive by looking at it, but she could only see that there were only grey or brown sprays and branches, and none showed any signs of even a tiny leaf-bud anywhere.

But she was *inside* the wonderful garden, and she could come through the door under the ivy any time, and she felt as if she had found a world all her own.

The sun was shining inside the four walls and the high arch of blue sky over this particular piece of Misselthwaite seemed even more brilliant and soft than it was over the moor. The robin flew down from his tree-top and hopped about or flew after her from one bush to another. He chirped a good deal and had a very busy air, as if he were showing her things. Everything was strange and silent, and she seemed to be hundreds of miles away from anyone, but somehow she did not feel lonely at all. All that troubled her was her wish that she knew whether all the roses were dead, or if perhaps some of them had lived and might put out leaves and buds as the weather got warmer. She did not want it to be a quite dead garden. If it were a quite alive garden, how wonderful it would be, and what thousands of roses would grow on every side!

Her skipping-rope had hung over her arm when she came in, and after she had walked about for a while she thought she would skip round the whole garden, stopping when she wanted to look at things. There seemed to have been grass paths here and there, and in one or two corners there were alcoves of evergreen with stone seats or tall moss-covered flower-urns in them.

As she came near the second of these alcoves she stopped skipping. There had once been a flowerbed in it, and she thought she saw something sticking out of the black earth – some sharp little pale green points. She remembered what Ben Weatherstaff had said, and she knelt down to look at them.

'Yes, they are tiny growing things and they *might* be crocuses or snowdrops or daffodils,' she whispered.

She bent very close to them and sniffed the fresh scent of the damp earth. She liked it very much.

'Perhaps there are some other ones coming up in

other places,' she said. 'I will go all over the garden and look.'

She did not skip, but walked. She went slowly and kept her eyes on the ground. She looked in the old border-beds and among the grass, and after she had gone round, trying to miss nothing, she had found ever so many more sharp, pale green points, and she had become quite excited again.

'It isn't a quite dead garden,' she cried out softly to herself. 'Even if the roses are dead, there are other things alive.'

She did not know anything about gardening, but the grass seemed so thick in some of the places where the green points were pushing their way through that she thought they did not seem to have room enough to grow. She searched about until she found a rather sharp piece of wood and knelt down and dug and weeded out the weeds and grass until she made nice little clear places around them.

'Now they look as if they could breathe,' she said, after she had finished with the first ones. 'I am going to do ever so many more. I'll do all I can see. If I haven't time today I can come tomorrow.'

She went from place to place, and dug and weeded, and enjoyed herself so immensely that she was led on from bed to bed and into the grass under the trees. The exercise made her so warm that she first threw her coat off, and then her hat, and without knowing it she was smiling down on to the grass and the pale green points all the time.

The robin was tremendously busy. He was very much pleased to see gardening begun on his own estate. He had often wondered at Ben Weatherstaff. Where gardening is done all sorts of delightful things to eat are turned up with the soil. Now here was this new kind of creature who was not half Ben's size and yet had had the sense to come into his garden and begin at once.

Mistress Mary worked in her garden until it was time to go to her midday dinner. In fact, she was rather late in remembering, and when she put on her coat and hat and picked up her skipping-rope, she could not believe that she had been working two or three hours. She had been actually happy all the time; and dozens and dozens of the tiny, pale green points were to be seen in cleared places, looking twice as cheerful as they had looked before when the grass and weeds had been smothering them.

'I shall come back this afternoon,' she said, looking all round at her new kingdom and speaking to the trees and the rose bushes as if they heard her.

AMANDA OWEN
(*b.* 1974)

Amanda Owen grew up in Huddersfield but was inspired by the James Herriot books to leave her town life behind and head to the countryside. After working as a freelance shepherdess, cow milker and alpaca shearer, she eventually settled down as a farmer's wife at Ravenseat in the Yorkshire Dales. She has recorded the ups and downs of rural life, with her husband and nine children, in two autobiographical volumes. In this extract she writes about her first farming job.

from The Yorkshire Shepherdess

WILD OATS AND WOOL SACKS

My first full-time farming job was milking cows on a family farm at Wakefield, and I soon realized I had to navigate a difficult path between two bosses who had different ideas about what I should be doing. There were actually two farms, and on one the old father ruled, and on the other his son, freshly back from agricultural college, was in charge. Or that was the theory: the old farmer would turn up and tell me to do things completely differently from the way his son had, only minutes before, told me to do them. The old fella wanted everything done the traditional way, like it always had been, and the young lad had lots of new ideas, which his father thought were plain daft. They disagreed over the simplest things.

For example: there were 130 cows to milk and usually about 25 calves to feed, and the son wanted me to wash the buckets, sterilize them and stand them in a line as he reckoned there was a danger that dirt could be transferred from one to another if they were stacked. Then the old chap would appear and ask what on earth I was doing with all the buckets spread out as they would get dirty, and were in the way and they should be stacked together. I was forever being lambasted by one of them because of something the other had told me to do. You could never do things right: one of them was always on your case. There were two YTS (the government's Youth Training Scheme) lads working there as well, and we were all permanently in the doghouse with one of our bosses. There was another old farmhand who had been there since the dawn of time, and it was a bit of a blokes' paradise: they'd never had a girl working there.

When I got the job I was told, 'Make sure thi brings thi bait box.'

I thought, Bait? What's fishing got to do with it?

I soon found out it meant 'lunch box'. We'd sit outside to eat if it was fine, but if it was raining – and it usually was – we'd sit inside a shed on plastic milk crates and tea chests. The tea chests were full of porn magazines. It was a bit off-putting trying to eat your sandwich with three chaps studying *Playboy*, but it never *really* bothered me. If you want to work in a world that has for centuries been traditionally male, you can't be indignant and feminist when you get a bit of banter or hear some crude talk.

It was hard work. I left home on my bike at 6 a.m. every morning to be there by 7 a.m., an hour's ride up and down hills. If I didn't take the bike, I had to travel on two buses, which took much longer. There was one thing for sure after I'd been on the farm all day: I could literally clear the bus, I smelt so bad, usually of silage – a smell that really sticks in your throat.

The job was seven days a week, but every third weekend I got what the farmer called my 'weekend off'. This was the worst time of all: I was still expected to do the morning and evening milking, so the only time I got off was a few hours in the middle. And it meant doing the journey twice a day, instead of once. I seemed to be on that bicycle saddle pedalling all day. No wonder I had no time for socializing with friends or going out on dates. By this time my school and college friends had gone their different ways. One was at Oxford, studying hard, and another was a trainee cashier at Lloyds Bank; others, too, had sensible, normal jobs. I didn't feel that I wasn't as good as them, but I was still a bit confused about everything. I liked the farm work, but the hours were crucifying, and I felt I hadn't quite got my life right yet.

The farm was part arable, which was something completely new to me. I spent hours shovelling grain into silos and grain lofts, then filling sacks with barley. I also had a combine harvester to grease up, 130 grease nipples to do every morning during the harvest. It was the old fellow's pride and joy, an ancient belt-driven piece of machinery, and he'd do spot checks to see that I'd greased it properly.

I was sent out with a hessian sack tied across my back to carefully pick the wild oats that were growing amongst the barley, and told to take my bait with me. Looking across the fields of golden, ripening barley, I could see the wild oats, their green panicles standing head and shoulders above the barley ears. At first glance it seemed there was only a handful of the weeds, but when I was crouching down in the field I could see the extent of their spread. No wonder he told me to take my bait. The upside of these long days in the fields was that I developed a golden tan like nothing you can buy in a tanning salon. The downside: it stopped at my welly tops.

Harvest time was very intensive: when the moisture meter registered the required grain dryness it was all hands on deck. Floodlights were rigged up in the fields and nobody stopped until all was safely gathered in. Although it was very hard work I felt that at least I was getting good practical experience. I learned how to set up an umbilical spreader, which is a long pipe to spread slurry on the fields using a tractor or a metal pulley contraption; how to use a power harrow to break up clods of soil to prepare the ground for planting; how to dehorn a calf and how to drive a tractor. I already knew how to drive a car, because Father had patiently taken me out to show me the ropes. Then I had one lesson with an instructor, just to refine the bits you need for the test, and I passed first time.

I think Mother and Father did wonder 'What on earth is she doing?', especially when I came home filthy and stinking. The truth is, I was right at the bottom of the food chain, the dogsbody who was expected to do anything, but I was happy to be working, and I was learning all the time. You had to start somewhere and, besides, there were other things going on at home that were more important than my career.

It was at this time, when I was eighteen, that my father died. For years he thought he had a stomach ulcer, and he'd been prescribed Gaviscon, an antacid used for indigestion. Eventually, when the pain got worse, his doctor sent him for tests and they discovered he had stomach cancer. He was quite ill by this stage and had to give up work. Eventually, he could no longer even tinker with his beloved motorbikes. That was the worst bit for him. It was heartbreaking to see him clearing out all the bikes and cataloguing the parts and spares that filled the garage, cellar and loft. I might have known my crankshafts from my con rods but there was a whole lot more stuff that he had accumulated over the years, and he was adamant that after he died we should not be hoodwinked by any unscrupulous buyers. Other than making us promise to never sell his compressor, he made every effort to get as much of his collection as possible sold to enthusiasts before he died. Mother had been working as a school dinner lady, and she had to give up work to look after him. Katie was twelve at the time, so it was a difficult period for all of us.

I was with Father when he died. He was at home and had been on a morphine drip for days. I am still haunted by it. It was such a strange experience, it felt like it wasn't really happening to me: dealing with the practicalities involved, ringing a doctor and a funeral director and, worst of all, having to go to Grandma's house and tell her that her son had died. I didn't want to go to the funeral, but Mother insisted. I had another argument with her:

'You're not going dressed as a Goth.'

'He wouldn't know me any other way. Anyway, the theme is black, I can't see your problem.'

I've hated funerals ever since, and I rarely go to them.

EMILY BRONTË
(1818–1848)

Wuthering Heights is a complex story, told through different narrators and covering different generations. It is filled with ghostly presences and visions, such as this early scene when Lockwood is visited by the spirit of Catherine Earnshaw in a nightmare. First published in 1847, the origins of *Wuthering Heights* are rooted in the Gothic novels of the eighteenth century, but the novel's strange power comes from a deep connection with the natural world. Emily Brontë's only novel is unlike anything which came before it – or since – and it defies categorization. It has a moral ambiguity which appeals to modern readers but repulsed its Victorian audiences, who were used to authors explicitly condemning their wicked characters. Heathcliff is driven by a diabolic revenge and Cathy is a passionate force of nature who evokes little sympathy. It is an uneasy read, which lingers in the memory and, like the description at the end of the novel of Heathcliff and Cathy's graves on the moors, it is hard to imagine 'unquiet slumbers for the sleepers in that quiet earth'.

from Wuthering Heights

I was lying in the oak closet, and I heard distinctly the gusty wind, and the driving of the snow; I heard, also, the fir bough repeat its teasing sound, and ascribed it to the right cause: but it annoyed me so much, that I resolved to silence it, if possible; and, I thought, I rose and endeavoured to unhasp the casement. The hook was soldered into the staple: a circumstance observed by me when awake, but forgotten. 'I must stop it, nevertheless!' I muttered, knocking my knuckles through the glass, and stretching an arm out to seize the importunate branch; instead of which, my fingers closed on the fingers of a little, ice-cold hand! The intense horror of nightmare came over me: I tried to draw back my arm, but the hand clung to it, and a most melancholy voice sobbed, 'Let me in – let me in!' 'Who are you?' I asked, struggling, meanwhile, to disengage myself. 'Catherine Linton,' it replied shiveringly (why did I think of *Linton*? I had read *Earnshaw* twenty times for Linton). 'I'm come home: I'd lost my way on the moor!' As it spoke, I discerned, obscurely, a child's face looking through the window. Terror made me cruel; and, finding it useless to attempt shaking the creature off, I pulled its wrist on to the broken pane, and rubbed it to and fro till the blood ran down and soaked the bedclothes: still it wailed, 'Let me in!' and maintained its tenacious gripe, almost maddening me with fear. 'How can I!' I said at length. 'Let *me* go, if you want me to let you in!' The fingers relaxed, I snatched mine through the hole, hurriedly piled the books up in a pyramid against it, and stopped my ears to exclude the lamentable prayer. I seemed to keep them closed above a quarter of an hour; yet, the instant I listened again, there was the doleful cry moaning on! 'Begone!' I shouted, 'I'll never let you in, not if you beg for twenty years.' 'It is twenty years,' mourned the voice: 'twenty years. I've been a waif for twenty years!' Thereat began a feeble scratching outside, and the pile of books moved as if thrust forward. I tried to jump up; but could not stir a limb; and so yelled aloud, in a frenzy of fright. To my confusion, I discovered the yell was not ideal: hasty footsteps approached my chamber door; somebody pushed it open, with a vigorous hand, and a light glimmered through the squares at the top of the bed. I sat shuddering yet, and wiping the perspiration from my forehead: the intruder appeared to hesitate, and muttered to himself. At last, he said in a half-whisper, plainly not expecting an answer, 'Is anyone here?' I considered it best to confess my presence; for I knew Heathcliff's accents, and feared he might search further, if I kept quiet. With this intention, I turned and opened the panels. I shall not soon forget the effect my action produced.

Heathcliff stood near the entrance, in his shirt and trousers; with a candle dripping over his fingers, and his face as white as the wall behind him. The first creak of the oak startled him like an electric shock: the light leaped from his hold to a distance of some feet, and his agitation was so extreme, that he could hardly pick it up.

'It is only your guest, sir,' I called out, desirous to spare him the humiliation of exposing his cowardice further. 'I had the misfortune to scream in my sleep, owing to a frightful nightmare. I'm sorry I disturbed you.'

PEOPLE

CHARLOTTE BRONTË
(1816–1855)

Jane Eyre by Charlotte Brontë is one of the best-known and best-loved nineteenth-century novels. It has provided a template for many a Gothic romantic novel since. The novel charts the 'poor, obscure, plain and little' Jane's search for self-worth and equality as she faces the challenges of a cruel schooling, based on Charlotte's own experiences at Cowan Bridge, and then a moral dilemma when Jane falls in love with Rochester, who has employed her as a governess, and who proposes marriage to Jane, despite having a wife who is locked away and is suffering from mental illness. In this extract, Jane encounters Rochester for the first time.

from Jane Eyre

The ground was hard, the air was still, my road was lonely; I walked fast till I got warm, and then I walked slowly to enjoy and analyse the species of pleasure brooding for me in the hour and situation. It was three o'clock; the church bell tolled as I passed under the belfry: the charm of the hour lay in its approaching dimness, in the low-gliding and pale-beaming sun. I was a mile from Thornfield, in a lane noted for wild roses in summer, for nuts and blackberries in autumn, and even now possessing a few coral treasures in hips and haws, but whose best winter delight lay in its utter solitude and leafless repose. If a breath of air stirred, it made no sound here; for there was not a holly, not an evergreen to rustle, and the stripped hawthorn and hazel bushes were as still as the white, worn stones which causewayed the middle of the path. Far and wide, on each side, there were only fields, where no cattle now browsed; and the little brown birds, which stirred occasionally in the hedge, looked like single russet leaves that had forgotten to drop.

This lane inclined uphill all the way to Hay; having reached the middle, I sat down on a stile which led thence into a field. Gathering my mantle about me, and sheltering my hands in my muff, I did not feel the cold, though it froze keenly; as was attested by a sheet of ice covering the causeway, where a little brooklet, now congealed, had overflowed after a rapid thaw some days since. From my seat I could look down on Thornfield: the grey and battlemented hall was the principal object in the vale below me; its woods and dark rookery rose against the west. I lingered till the sun went down amongst the trees, and sank crimson and clear behind them. I then turned eastward.

On the hilltop above me sat the rising moon; pale yet as a cloud, but brightening momentarily, she looked over Hay, which, half lost in trees, sent up a blue smoke from its few chimneys: it was yet a mile distant, but in the absolute hush I could hear plainly its thin murmurs of life. My ear, too, felt the flow of currents; in what dales and depths I could not tell: but there were many hills beyond Hay, and doubtless many becks threading their passes. That evening calm betrayed alike the tinkle of the nearest streams, the sough of the most remote.

A rude noise broke on these fine ripplings and whisperings, at once so far away and so clear: a positive tramp, tramp, a metallic clatter, which effaced the soft wave-wanderings; as, in a picture, the solid mass of a crag, or the rough boles of a great oak, drawn in dark and strong on the foreground, efface the aerial distance of azure hill, sunny horizon, and blended clouds where tint melts into tint.

The din was on the causeway: a horse was coming; the windings of the lane yet hid it, but it approached. I was just leaving the stile; yet, as the path was narrow, I sat still to let it go by. In those days I was young, and all sorts of fancies bright and dark tenanted my mind: the memories of nursery stories were there amongst other rubbish; and when they recurred, maturing youth added to them a vigour and vividness beyond what childhood could give. As this horse approached, and as I watched for it to appear through the dusk, I remembered certain of Bessie's tales, wherein figured a North-of-England spirit called a 'Gytrash,' which, in the form of horse, mule, or large dog, haunted solitary ways, and sometimes came upon belated travellers, as this horse was now coming upon me.

It was very near, but not yet in sight; when, in addition to the tramp, tramp, I heard a rush under the hedge, and close down by the hazel stems glided a great dog, whose black and white colour made him a distinct object against the trees. It was exactly one form of Bessie's Gytrash – a lion-like creature with long hair and a huge head: it passed me, however, quietly enough; not staying to look up, with strange pretercanine eyes, in my face, as I half expected it would. The horse followed – a tall steed, and on its back a rider. The man, the human being, broke the spell at once. Nothing ever rode the Gytrash: it was always alone; and goblins, to my notions, though they might tenant the dumb carcasses of beasts, could scarce covet shelter in the commonplace human form. No Gytrash was this – only a traveller taking the short cut to Millcote. He passed, and I went on; a few steps, and I turned: a sliding sound and an exclamation of 'What the deuce is to do now?' and a clattering tumble, arrested my attention. Man and horse were down; they had slipped on the sheet of ice which glazed the causeway. The dog came bounding back, and seeing his master in a predicament, and hearing the horse groan, barked till the evening hills echoed the sound, which was deep in proportion to his magnitude. He snuffed round the prostrate group, and then he ran up to me; it was all he could do – there was no other help at hand to summon. I obeyed him, and walked down to the traveller, by this time struggling himself free of his steed. His efforts were so vigorous, I thought he could not be much hurt; but I asked him the question – 'Are you injured, sir?'

I think he was swearing, but am not certain; however, he was pronouncing some formula which prevented him from replying to me directly.

'Can I do anything?' I asked again.

'You must just stand on one side,' he answered as he rose, first to his knees, and then to his feet. I did; whereupon began a heaving, stamping, clattering process, accompanied by a barking and baying which removed me effectually some yards' distance; but I would not be driven quite away till I saw the event. This was finally fortunate; the horse was reestablished, and the dog was silenced with a 'Down, Pilot!' The traveller now, stooping, felt his foot and leg, as if trying whether they were sound; apparently something ailed them, for he halted to the stile whence I had just risen, and sat down.

I was in the mood for being useful, or at least officious, I think, for I now drew near him again.

'If you are hurt, and want help, sir, I can fetch someone either from Thornfield Hall or from Hay.'

'Thank you: I shall do: I have no broken bones – only a sprain;' and again he stood up and tried his foot, but the result extorted an involuntary 'Ugh!'

Something of daylight still lingered, and the moon was waxing bright: I could see him plainly. His figure was enveloped in a riding cloak, fur collared and steel clasped; its details were not apparent, but I traced the general points of middle height and considerable breadth of chest. He had a dark face, with stern features and a heavy brow; his eyes and gathered eyebrows looked ireful and thwarted just now; he was past youth, but had not reached middle-age; perhaps he might be thirty-five. I felt no fear of him, and but little shyness. Had he been a handsome, heroic-looking young gentleman, I should not have dared to stand thus questioning him against his will, and offering my services unasked. I had hardly ever seen a handsome youth; never in my life spoken to one. I had a theoretical reverence and homage for beauty, elegance, gallantry, fascination; but had I met those qualities incarnate in masculine shape, I should have known instinctively that they neither had nor could have sympathy with anything in me, and should have shunned them as one would fire, lightning, or anything else that is bright but antipathetic.

If even this stranger had smiled and been good-humoured to me when I addressed him; if he had put off my offer of assistance gaily and with thanks, I should have gone on my way and not felt any vocation to renew enquiries: but the frown, the roughness of the traveller, set me at my ease: I retained my station when he waved to me to go, and announced – 'I cannot think of leaving you, sir, at so late an hour, in this solitary lane, till I see you are fit to mount your horse.'

He looked at me when I said this; he had hardly turned his eyes in my direction before.

'I should think you ought to be at home yourself,' said he, 'if you have a home in this neighbourhood: where do you come from?'

'From just below; and I am not at all afraid of being out late when it is moonlight: I will run over to Hay for you with pleasure, if you wish it: indeed, I am going there to post a letter.'

'You live just below – do you mean at that house with the battlements?' pointing to Thornfield Hall, on which the moon cast a hoary gleam, bringing it out distinct and pale from the woods, that, by contrast with the western sky, now seemed one mass of shadow.

'Yes, sir.'

'Whose house is it?'

'Mr Rochester's.'

'Do you know Mr Rochester?'

'No, I have never seen him.'

'He is not resident, then?'

'No.'

'Can you tell me where he is?'

'I cannot.'

'You are not a servant at the hall, of course. You are –' He stopped, ran his eye over my dress, which, as usual, was quite simple: a black merino cloak, a black beaver bonnet; neither of them half fine enough for a lady's maid. He seemed puzzled to decide what I was; I helped him.

'I am the governess.'

'Ah, the governess!' he repeated; 'deuce take me, if I had not forgotten! The governess!' and again my raiment underwent scrutiny. In two minutes he rose from the stile: his face expressed pain when he tried to move.

'I cannot commission you to fetch help,' he said; 'but you may help me a little yourself, if you will be so kind.'

'Yes, sir.'

'You have not an umbrella that I can use as a stick?'

'No.'

'Try to get hold of my horse's bridle and lead him to me: you are not afraid?'

I should have been afraid to touch a horse when alone, but when told to do it, I was disposed to obey. I put down my muff on the stile, and went up to the tall steed; I endeavoured to catch the bridle, but it was a spirited thing, and would not let me come near its head; I made effort on effort, though in vain: meantime, I was mortally afraid of its trampling forefeet. The traveller waited and watched for some time, and at last he laughed.

'I see,' he said, 'the mountain will never be brought to Mahomet, so all you can do is to aid Mahomet to go to the mountain; I must beg of you to come here.'

I came. 'Excuse me,' he continued: 'necessity compels me to make you useful.' He laid a heavy hand on my shoulder, and leaning on me with some stress, limped to his horse. Having once caught the bridle, he mastered it directly and sprang to his saddle; grimacing grimly as he made the effort, for it wrenched his sprain.

'Now,' said he, releasing his under lip from a hard bite, 'just hand me my whip; it lies there under the hedge.'

I sought it and found it.

'Thank you; now make haste with the letter to Hay, and return as fast as you can.'

A touch of a spurred heel made his horse first start and rear, and then bound away; the dog rushed in his traces; all three vanished,

'Like heath that, in the wilderness,
The wild wind whirls away.'

CÆDMON
(c. 657–684)

Cædmon is one of the earliest known English poets. He was a monk who resided at the monastery of Streonæshalch, now known as Whitby Abbey, where he cared for the animals. According to the eighth-century historian the Venerable Bede, Cædmon was a brother particularly remarkable for 'the Grace of God, who was wont to make religious verses, so that whatever was interpreted to him out of scripture, he soon after put the same into poetical expressions of much sweetness and humility in Old English, which was his native language. By his verse the minds of many were often excited to despise the world, and to aspire to heaven.'

Cædmon's only known surviving work is 'Cædmon's Hymn', the nine-line praise poem in honour of God.

Here is a modern version, translated from the Old English.

Cædmon's Hymn

Now [we] must honour the guardian of heaven,
the might of the architect and his purpose,
the work of the father of glory as he the
   beginnings of wonders
established, the eternal lord,
He first created for the children of men
heaven as a roof, the holy creator
Then the middle earth, the guardian of mankind
the eternal lord, afterwards appointed
the lands of men, the Lord almighty.

ANNE BRONTË
(1820–1849)

From early childhood, the Brontës wrote poems and illustrated stories, initially creating tiny hand-made 'little books' less than a couple of inches high telling tales of a private world peopled by characters based on a set of toy soldiers their father brought home for Branwell in 1826. By the time the sisters self-published a collection of poems, they had served a twenty-year literary apprenticeship. Many of the poems selected for the 1846 edition of their poetry were reworked versions of those rooted in the children's imaginary worlds: Angria, a Byronic land which Charlotte and Branwell worked on together, and Gondal, created by Emily and Anne, where powerful women ruled. In her poem 'The Consolation', Anne, at the time working away as a governess, dreams of her home at Haworth.

The Consolation

Though bleak these woods, and
   damp the ground
With fallen leaves so thickly strown,
And cold the wind that wanders round
With wild and melancholy moan;

There *is* a friendly roof, I know,
Might shield me from the wintry blast;
There is a fire, whose ruddy glow
Will cheer me for my wanderings past.

And so, though still, where'er I go,
Cold stranger-glances meet my eye;
Though, when my spirit sinks in woe,
Unheeded swells the unbidden sigh;

Though solitude, endured too long,
Bids youthful joys too soon decay,
Makes mirth a stranger to my tongue,
And overclouds my noon of day;

When kindly thoughts, that would have way,
Flow back discouraged to my breast; –
I know there *is*, though far away,
A home where heart and soul may rest.

Warm hands are there, that, clasped in mine,
The warmer heart will not belie;
While mirth, and truth, and friendship shine
In smiling lip and earnest eye.

The ice that gathers round my heart
May there be thawed; and sweetly, then,
The joys of youth, that now depart,
Will come to cheer my soul again.

Though far I roam, that thought shall be
My hope, my comfort, everywhere;
While such a home remains to me,
My heart shall never know despair!

BRAM STOKER
(1847–1912)

Whitby Abbey, which still stands like a Gothic sentinel, is where Dracula takes his first victim on British soil. This is Lucy Westenra, whose midnight encounter with Dracula at the abbey is recorded by Mina Murray in her diary. By supernatural means, the Count has lured the girl from her bed to rendezvous with him at the abbey.

from Dracula

11 August, *3 a.m.* – Diary again. No sleep now, so I may as well write. I am too agitated to sleep. We have had such an adventure, such an agonising experience. I fell asleep as soon as I had closed my diary . . . Suddenly I became broad awake, and sat up, with a horrible sense of fear upon me, and of some feeling of emptiness around me. The room was dark, so I could not see Lucy's bed; I stole across and felt for her. The bed was empty. I lit a match, and found that she was not in the room. The door was shut, but not locked, as I had left it. I feared to wake her mother, who has been more than usually ill lately, so threw on some clothes and got ready to look for her. As I was leaving the room it struck me that the clothes she wore might give me some clue to her dreaming intention. Dressing-gown would mean house; dress, outside. Dressing-gown and dress were both in their places. 'Thank God,' I said to myself, 'she cannot be far, as she is only in her nightdress.' I ran downstairs and looked in the sitting-room. Not there! Then I looked in all the other open rooms of the house, with an ever-growing fear chilling my heart. Finally I came to the hall-door and found it open. It was not wide open, but the catch of the lock had not caught. The people of the house are careful to lock the door every night, so I feared that Lucy must have gone out as she was. There was no time to think of what might

happen; a vague, overmastering fear obscured all details. I took a big, heavy shawl and ran out. The clock was striking one as I was in the Crescent, and there was not a soul in sight. I ran along the North Terrace, but could see no sign of the white figure which I expected. At the edge of the West Cliff above the pier I looked across the harbour to the East Cliff, in the hope or fear – I don't know which – of seeing Lucy in our favourite seat. There was a bright full moon, with heavy black, driving clouds, which threw the whole scene into a fleeting diorama of light and shade as they sailed across. For a moment or two I could see nothing, as the shadow of a cloud obscured St Mary's Church and all around it. Then as the cloud passed I could see the ruins of the Abbey coming into view; and as the edge of a narrow band of light as sharp as a sword-cut moved along, the church and the churchyard became gradually visible. Whatever my expectation was, it was not disappointed, for there, on our favourite seat, the silver light of the moon struck a half-reclining figure, snowy white. The coming of the cloud was too quick for me to see much, for shadow shut down on light almost immediately; but it seemed to me as though something dark stood behind the seat where the white figure shone, and bent over it. What it was, whether man or beast, I could not tell; I did not wait to catch another glance, but flew down the steep steps to the pier and along by the fish-market to the bridge, which was the only way to reach the East Cliff. The town seemed as dead, for not a soul did I see; I rejoiced that it was so, for I wanted no witness of poor Lucy's condition. The time and distance seemed endless, and my knees trembled and my breath came laboured as I toiled up the endless steps to the Abbey. I must have gone fast, and yet it seemed to me as if my feet were weighted with lead, and as though every joint in my body were rusty. When I got almost to the top I could see the seat and the white figure, for I was now close enough to distinguish it even through the spells of shadow. There was undoubtedly something, long and black, bending over the half-reclining white figure. I called in fright, 'Lucy! Lucy!' and something raised a head, and from where I was I could see a white face and red, gleaming eyes. Lucy did not answer, and I ran on to the entrance of the churchyard. As I entered, the church was between me and the seat, and for a minute or so I lost sight of her. When I came in view again the cloud had passed, and the moonlight struck so brilliantly that I could see Lucy half reclining with her head lying over the back of the seat. She was quite alone, and there was not a sign of any living thing about.

When I bent over her I could see that she was still asleep. Her lips were parted, and she was breathing – not softly, as usual with her, but in long, heavy gasps, as though striving to get her lungs full at every breath. As I came close, she put up her hand in her sleep and pulled the collar of her nightdress close round her throat. Whilst she did so there came a little shudder through her, as though she felt the cold. I flung the warm shawl over her, and drew the edges tight round her neck, for I dreaded lest she should get some deadly chill from the night air, unclad as she was. I feared to wake her all at once, so, in order to have my hands free that I might help her, I fastened the shawl at her throat with a big safety-pin; but I must have been clumsy in my anxiety and pinched or pricked her with it, for by and by, when her breathing became quieter, she put her hand to her throat again and moaned. When I had her carefully wrapped up I put my shoes on her feet, and then began very gently to wake her. At first she did not respond; but gradually she became more and more uneasy in her sleep, moaning and sighing occasionally. At last, as time was passing fast, and for many other reasons, I wished to get her home at once, I shook her more forcibly, till finally she opened her eyes and awoke. She did not seem surprised to see me, as, of course, she did not realise all at once where she was. Lucy always wakes prettily, and even at such a time, when her body must have been chilled with cold, and her mind somewhat appalled at waking unclad in a churchyard at night, she did not lose her grace. She trembled a little, and clung to me; when I told her to come at once with me home she rose without a word, with the obedience of a child. As we passed along, the gravel hurt my feet, and Lucy noticed me wince. She stopped and wanted to insist upon my taking my shoes; but I would not. However, when we got to the pathway outside the churchyard, where there was a puddle of water remaining from the storm, I daubed my feet with mud, using each foot in turn on the other, so that as we went home no one, in case we should meet anyone, should notice my bare feet.

Fortune favoured us, and we got home without meeting a soul. Once we saw a man, who seemed not quite sober, passing along a street in front of us; but we hid in a door till he had disappeared up an opening such as there are here, steep little closes, or 'wynds', as they call them in Scotland. My heart beat so loud all the time that sometimes I thought I should faint. I was filled with anxiety about Lucy, not only for her health, lest she should suffer from the exposure, but for her reputation in case the story should get wind. When we got in, and had washed our feet, and had said a prayer of thankfulness together, I tucked her into bed. Before falling asleep she asked – even implored – me not to say a word to anyone, even her mother, about her sleep-walking adventure. I hesitated at first to promise; but on thinking of the state of her mother's health, and how the knowledge of such a thing would fret her, and thinking, too, of how such a story might become distorted – nay, infallibly would – in case it should leak out I thought it wiser to do so. I hope I did right. I have locked the door, and the key is tied to my wrist, so perhaps I shall not be again disturbed. Lucy is sleeping soundly; the reflex of the dawn is high and far over the sea . . .

Same day, noon – All goes well. Lucy slept till I woke her, and seemed not to have even changed her side. The adventure of the night does not seem to have harmed her; on the contrary, it has benefited her, for she looks better this morning than she has done for weeks. I was sorry to notice that my clumsiness with the safety-pin hurt her. Indeed, it might have been serious, for the skin of her throat was pierced. I must have pinched up a piece of loose skin and have transfixed it, for there are two little red points like pinpricks, and on the band of her nightdress was a drop of blood. When I apologised and was concerned about it, she laughed and petted me, and said she did not even feel it. Fortunately it cannot leave a scar, as it is so tiny.

IAN MCMILLAN
(*b.* 1956)

Ian McMillan is a Yorkshire poet, writer, broadcaster and performer, whose work exudes 'Yorkshireness'. He is known as the Bard of Barnsley and is regarded as 'poet in residence' to his hometown football club, Barnsley FC. The man himself speaks with a broad, rich Barnsley accent which seems to infiltrate his verse. His deceptively simple poetry is often an amalgam of humour, wisdom, nostalgia and moral perceptions, and has a strange quirkiness which speaks to both adults and children.

No Bread

I wish I'd made a list,
I forgot to get the bread.
If I forget it again
I'll be dead.

We had blank and butter pudding,
beans on zip.
Boiled eggs with deserters,
no chip butty: just chip.

I wish I'd made a list,
I forgot to get the bread.
My mam got the empty bread bin
and wrapped it round my head.

Our jam sarnies were just jam
floating on the air.
We spread butter on the table
cos the bread wasn't there.

My mam says if I run away
she knows I won't be missed,
not like the bread was . . .
I wish I'd made a list!

from 'Enjoy the Game'

If Yorkshire isn't just a celebration of the past then I need to find something that can be an emblem of the past and the present and the future. It seems to me that one of the main things Yorkshire defines itself through is sport: football, rugby, cricket, solitary hours fishing, the rapid castanets of dominoes, the darts that leave your hand as winners and then the air decides otherwise, the pigeon flyers that take their baskets to remote spots and practise the art of liberation, the cyclists who, particularly since the Tour de France, whirr up hills in the wrong gear or whizz down resisting the urge to whoop. Maybe Yorkshire itself is a game; a board game where Mayfair is Harrogate and Old Kent Road is wherever you remember as scruffy before you moved away to the suburbs.

If I'm looking for a metaphor for Yorkshire, then sport is it, and that's because competitiveness pounds in the Yorkshireman and Yorkshirewoman's veins, running as fast as it can alongside our blood to keep up, and sometimes overtaking it. We like to win and don't mind, in the current sporting parlance, 'winning ugly'; and if I dig a little deeper then it becomes obvious to me that I'm not just talking about sport. Our marrows and our leeks and our onions have to be the biggest and the best; our station platforms have to be the coldest; our caps have to be the flattest; our accents have to be the closest to the way the whole of the country spoke in a mythical past; our polished anecdotes of poverty and despair have to wrench more tears from the listener than any slapdash Lancashire tale of cold and misery.

Let's face it: the famous Monty Python 'Four Yorkshiremen' sketch was a fly-on-the-wall documentary rather than a piece of observational comedy.

Our love for organised sport is partly to do with our industrial past, when cricket and rugby and football teams were organised alongside the brass bands and the choirs by the factory and the steelworks and the pit. I don't like the cliché 'work hard, play hard' but that's what it was. After grafting next to someone for eight hours on the coal face you tried to score a penalty past him or knock a six all the way into his allotment. After all, sport is about competition and communality and self-expression, and that could be the Holy Trinity of Yorkshireness.

The idea that you have to be born in Yorkshire to play cricket for the county has more or less evaporated now, but the sentiment hangs on, often in tap rooms on long autumn afternoons at the end of the season, or at bus stops at the opposite point of the year, populated by knots of men and women who carry flasks and plastic sandwich boxes like badges of honour.

So if sport is the sweaty and liniment-soaked prism through which Yorkshire views the world and its place in the wider universe and, as a season-ticket holder at the mighty, mighty, Barnsley FC I can agree with that, then where do I start with Yorkshire sport?

At times it feels like this county is glued together by a sporting event that has happened, is happening, or is just about to happen, and that's fine by me.

No Yorkshire person will allow any other Yorkshire person (or anybody else in hearing distance for that matter) to forget that, if Yorkshire was a country, it would have come twelfth in the medal table at the 2012 Olympics; Yorkshire feet pounded tracks and part-sturdy, part-fragile boats were rowed through water with the aid of Yorkshire shoulders and Yorkshire legs cycled till their thighs burned and Yorkshire arms flung sharp javelins and Yorkshire bottoms rode on their horses through the warming air and Yorkshire fists knocked opponents for six. The golden names ring out like bells: Ennis, Adams, Campbell, Brownlee, Clancy, Triggs-Hodge, Copeland. Their golden pillarboxes light up the Yorkshire-scape, reminding us of glory as they catch the evening light and the morning sun. Eat that, Lancashire! Chew on that, Sir Bradley Wiggins, you off-comed 'un! And, as the *Huddersfield Examiner* reminded us recently in a chortlingly joyous article, Yorkshire even won the space race, with Helen Sharman from Sheffield being the first British person to orbit Yorkshire and the earth. How's the Lancashire space-race going? Can I lend you some rubber bands and string? Gaaaaah!

(That last word embarrassed me. I'm sorry. I didn't mean to go Gaaaaah! and stick my face right next to yours, my eyes bulging and my chin, and then yours, flecked with spittle. After all, this is a respectable socio-cultural book. It's not a crowded pub half an hour after the match has finished. It's just that sport makes all Yorkshire people very, very competitive indeed. I'm not normally like this, Officer. This is the first time it's happened to me. It won't happen again.)

SIMON ARMITAGE
(*b.* 1965)

Simon Armitage was born in 1965 in the rural village of Marsden, near Huddersfield. He began his working life as a probation officer in Greater Manchester. He has written poetry since the age of ten and had his first book of poems, *Zoom!*, published in 1989. As his fame and success grew, he left the probation service in 1994 and devoted his professional life to writing, extending his range to writing novels, plays and essays. He has received numerous awards for his poetry and in 2019 he was appointed Poet Laureate. Armitage still lives in the Huddersfield area, a staunch supporter of the local football team. His often darkly comic poetry is influenced by the work of Ted Hughes, W. H. Auden and Philip Larkin. As a reviewer for PoetryArchive.org observed, 'With his acute eye for modern life, Armitage is an updated version of Wordsworth's "man talking to men".'

Hitcher

I'd been tired, under
the weather, but the ansaphone kept screaming:
One more sick-note, mister, and you're finished. Fired.
I thumbed a lift to where the car was parked.
A Vauxhall Astra. It was hired.

I picked him up in Leeds.
He was following the sun to west from east
with just a toothbrush and the good earth for a bed.
    The truth,
he said, was blowin' in the wind,
or round the next bend.

I let him have it
on the top road out of Harrogate – once
with the head, then six times with the krooklok
in the face – and didn't even swerve.
I dropped it into third

and leant across
to let him out, and saw him in the mirror
bouncing off the kerb, then disappearing down
    the verge.
We were the same age, give or take a week.
He'd said he liked the breeze

to run its fingers
through his hair. It was twelve noon.
The outlook for the day was moderate to fair.
Stitch that, I remember thinking,
you can walk from there.

BARRY HINES
(1939–2016)

A Kestrel for a Knave, Barry Hines' powerful, ground-breaking novel, continues to have an emotional resonance for teenagers and adults with its heartbreaking story of survival in the tough, joyless world of an impoverished mining community. Hines was born in such a village near Barnsley in South Yorkshire and drew on a great deal of the atmosphere and background detail from his own youth to infuse the narrative. It is the story of Billy Casper, a troubled teenager who is treated as a failure at school, ignored by his mother and bullied by his brother. But when he finds Kes, a young kestrel, his life changes. The bird gives Billy a purpose in life and he identifies with her silent strength and independence. Kes inspires in him the trust and love that nothing else can. In learning how to train the bird and the care and patience needed for such a task, he shows that he is not the stupid wastrel that his teachers and family think he is.

from A Kestrel for a Knave

He unlocked the shed door, slipped inside and closed it quietly behind him. The hawk was perched on a branch which had been wedged between the walls towards the back of the shed. The only other furniture in the shed were two shelves, one fixed behind the bars of the door, the other high up on one wall. The walls and ceiling were whitewashed, and the floor had been sprinkled with a thick layer of dry sand, sprinkled thicker beneath the perch and the shelves. The shelf on the door was marked with two dried mutes, both thick and white, with a central deposit of faeces as crozzled and black as the burnt ends of matches.

Billy approached the hawk slowly, regarding it obliquely, clucking and chanting softly, 'Kes Kes Kes.' The hawk bobbed her head and shifted along the perch. Billy held out his gauntlet and offered her a scrap of beef. She reached forward and grasped it with her beak, and tried to pull it from his glove. Billy gripped the beef tightly between forefinger and thumb; and in order to obtain more leverage, the hawk stepped on to his fist. He allowed her to take the beef, then replaced her on the perch, touching the backs of her legs against the wood so that she stepped backwards on to it. He dipped into the leather satchel at his hip and offered her a fresh scrap; this time holding it just out of range of her reaching beak. She bobbed her head and tippled forward slightly, regained balance, then glanced about, uncertain, like someone up on the top board for the first time.

'Come on, Kes. Come on then.'

He stood still. The hawk looked at the meat, then jumped on to the glove and took it. Billy smiled and replaced it with a tough strip of beef, and as the hawk busied herself with it, he attached a swivel to the ends of the jesses dangling from her legs, slipped the jesses between the first and second fingers of his glove, and felt into his bag for the leash. The hawk looked up from her feeding. Billy rubbed his finger and thumb to make the meat move between them, and as the hawk attended to it again, he threaded the leash through the lower ring of the swivel and pulled it all the way through until the knot at the other end snagged on the ring. He completed the security by looping the leash twice round his glove and tying the end round his little finger.

He walked to the door and slowly pushed it open. The hawk looked up, and as he moved out into the full light, her eyes seemed to expand, her body contract as she flattened her feathers. She bobbed her head, once, twice, then bated, throwing herself sideways off his glove and hanging upside down, thrashing her wings and screaming. Billy waited for her to stop, then placed his hand gently under her breast and lifted her back on to the glove. She bated again; and again, and each time Billy lifted her carefully back up, until finally she stayed up, beak half open, panting, glaring round.

'What's up then? What's a matter with you, Kes? Anybody'd think you'd never been out before.'

The hawk roused her feathers and bent to her meat, her misdemeanours apparently forgotten.

Billy walked her round the garden, speaking quietly to her all the time. Then he turned up the path at the side of the house and approached the front gate, watching the hawk for her reactions. A car approached. The hawk tensed, watched it pass, then resumed her meal as it sped away up the avenue. On the opposite pavement a little boy, pedalling a tricycle round in tight circles, looked up and saw them, immediately unwound and drove straight off the pavement, making the tin mudguards clank as the wheels jonked down into the gutter. Billy held the hawk away from him, anticipating a bate, but she scarcely glanced up at the sound, or at the boy as he cycled towards them and hutched his tricycle up on to the pavement.

'Oo that's a smasher. What is it?'

'What tha think it is?'

'Is it an owl?'

'It's a kestrel.'

'Where you got it from?'

'Found it.'

'Is it tame?'

'It's trained. I've trained it.'

Billy pointed to himself, and smiled across at the hawk.

'Don't it look fierce?'

'It is.'

'Does it kill things and eat 'em?'

'Course it does. It kills little kids on bikes.'

The boy laughed without smiling.

'It don't.'

'What's tha think that is it's eating now then?'

'It's only a piece of meat.'

'It's a piece o' leg off a kid it caught yesterday. When it catches 'em it sits on their handlebars and rips 'em to pieces. Eyes first.'

The boy looked down at the chrome handlebars and began to swing them from side to side, making the front wheel describe a steady arc like a windscreen wiper.

'I'll bet I dare stroke it.'

'Tha'd better not.'

'I'll bet I dare.'

'It'll have thi hand off if tha tries.'

The boy stood up, straddling the tricycle frame, and slowly lifted one hand towards the hawk. She mantled her wings over the meat, then struck out with her scaly yellow legs, screaming, and raking at the hand with her talons. The boy jerked his arm back with such force that its momentum carried his whole body over the tricycle and on to the ground. He scrambled up, as wide-eyed as the hawk, mounted, and pedalled off down the pavement, his legs whirring like bees' wings.

Billy watched him go, then opened the gate and walked up the avenue. He crossed at the top and walked down the other side to the cul-de-sac, round, and back up to his own house. And all the way round people stared, some crossing the avenue for a closer look, others glancing back. And the hawk, alert to every movement, returned their stares until they turned away and passed on.

Dorothy Una Ratcliffe

Life's Like a Fair

Life's like a Fair: a vast of work afore
A few hours' fun;
An' lang ere stars have wested ower t'moor
Light's out, all's done:
But to us each, according to our daring,
Time gives some Fairing.

MARY TAYLOR
(1817–1893)

The unconventional daughter of the politically radical Taylors of Red House in Gomersal, Mary Taylor became a feminist essayist in later life, a pioneering spirit who believed in the need for women to be independent and earn their own living. Mary was a lifelong friend of novelist Charlotte Brontë, inspiring her with 'a strong wish for wings', and to travel to Brussels in the early 1840s to further her education. Mary supported her friend's self-belief, and encouraged her to find her own powerful feminist voice as a writer. Charlotte used the Taylor family as the basis for the Yorkes in her novel *Shirley* (1849). *Miss Miles: A Tale of Yorkshire Life Sixty Years Ago* (1890) was written over a period of several decades and is Mary Taylor's only novel. Against a backdrop of poverty and the challenges faced by the mill communities of West Yorkshire, she explores the restrictions of the 'duty' of women, female self-sufficiency, and the courage to defy conventions of the time.

from Miss Miles

That sort of structure indefinitely called a mill has the power of gathering round it a kind of architecture more useful than ornamental. Trim gentility and retired leisure never seek its neighbourhood, and the picturesque cottages with diamond-paned windows, many-coloured thatch, and earthen floors, disappear under its influence. Their place is taken by weather-tight buildings with slated roofs, stone floors, and sash windows—repulsive to aestheticism, but cheering to the eyes of real philanthropists.

Such a change was passing over the village of Repton sixty years ago. It lay in a narrow valley in the West Riding of Yorkshire, with a stream and a lane running down the middle of it. On each side of these were green fields stretching upwards towards the heather that covered the high land for miles round. A road, still called the New Road, crossed the lane at right angles connecting the two nearest towns. On one side of the valley stood the great house of the landowner, Mr. Everard—whose necessities had made him let the ground for the mill—and the church and the vicarage were opposite on the other. Somewhat higher up the valley was the new chapel, and after this, perhaps, the most important building was the shop at the corner made by the lane and the road.

All this lay wrapped in December snow when our

story opens. A thick fog had covered it all day, but at dusk a keen north wind had swept the valley, and the frost made the burr of the clogs and the shouts of the children sound loud and clear. As the lights began to appear in the windows, a small crowd collected round the door of the shop where John Miles and his wife were prepared to serve till midnight, for it was Saturday, and it was a good year, and it was near to Christmas, and for all these reasons everyone was determined to spend their money.

It had not been always so with this isolated village, nor with England generally for the fifty years before. The scanty population of the country lived thinly scattered on the barren land. They grew their own oatmeal and bacon, and, perhaps, milk, and wanted little else. Towards the end of the eighteenth century three bad harvests followed in succession. In January, 1800, a bullock was roasted whole on the ice of the Thames, and the hills of the West Riding were covered in June with deep snow. The poor were in famine; rents were not paid. Many a wealthy family came down in the world, and many of the class below them were brought face to face with poverty. There was discontent among the starving people that the rulers thought dangerous; no one could say why it came, and no one could find a remedy.

It was in this year that a strange man came to the great house wanting a strange thing. He would like to buy, or lease, a few fields near the Beck and build a mill there. He was no gentleman in appearance, and his speech would have been unintelligible to anyone not born in the neighbourhood. Even in his own dialect he was not fluent enough to make Mr. Everard understand how he hoped to be able to give five times the old rent for the fields and yet drive a profitable trade.

But for years Mr. Everard had gone downhill. Rents were lower, burdens heavier, and prospects darker. He consented to lease the fields—not to sell them. Oh, no! they should come back to his family some time, though he might be dead and gone. His successors might even pull down the mill and restore the land to its old condition, when the good times came back again.

So the mill rose and prospered, in ugly proximity to the great house, the church, and the vicarage. The "trim gentility" of the place somehow hated it more than it deserved, for they had not the eyes to see its compensating good qualities. The poor took to it, fully appreciating the higher wages, and not caring in the least about the ugliness, nor even the dirt and smoke.

There was another cause for the enmity that then existed between the upper classes and the lower through the country.

It has been written with authority that had it not been for Wesley and Whitfield the name of Christ would have been unknown in that part of Yorkshire. Before Wesley, the little earnest religion there was existed among some sort of conventiclers, who were fined for meeting, fined for not going to church, and otherwise thwarted and oppressed.

Perhaps partly by this means the lukewarm and time-serving members were winnowed out of the little flock that had kept their Puritan proclivities, and they remained united and earnest. With immense difficulty they succeeded in building a small chapel—an eyesore and a wickedness to the vicar of the parish—and, after the mill had brought comparative prosperity, this was succeeded by a much larger one. Chapel-going became the fashion, and if the religion was not so earnest or so fruitful in good works as it ought to have been, why, it is not the first time such a thing has been true of churches, established or otherwise. The population, as a whole, were in opposition—in religion, because the only sincerity known to them had been among the Dissenters; in politics, because the vicar was zealously loyal and Tory, which in those days was almost the same thing. They were triumphant when the mill was in full work, and not docile when they were in want. These times came alternately, but not many of them learnt to minimize the effect of the one by the other.

On this particular Saturday before Christmas, in the house or living-room behind the shop, Sarah Miles was "cleaning up." She had washed the floor, replaced the chairs, and dusted the furniture, and now prepared to end her labours by washing the door-step. As she opened the door, she took a look up the lane and down the lane, sure of seeing someone she knew, and probably someone to speak to. She soon made out a girl of her own age standing outside the crowd and peering into the shop. She called to her—

"Eh, Harriet, lass!"

To whom thus Harriet—

"Sarah, haven't ye done yet? Jim Sugden an' me's been teeming water down ever sin drinkin' time, and it's t' grandest slide ye ever seed i' yer life!"

"I'm comin'," Sarah shouted, as she swept the steps with her cloth and then dashed the water into the open drain, and gently deposited the pail within the door.

Then, drying her bare arms on her canvas pinafore, she joined the boys and girls at the corner. She and Harriet were the two tallest; nearly fourteen, and well-grown, fine lasses, in dark-blue print, rough pinafores, and fuzzy hair.

"Here's Sarah!" shouted someone, and was nearly pushed down in the snow by Sarah for his zeal.

"Cannot ye hod yer din?" she said. "Mother'll hear ye!"

Then they all tramped up the hill, Sarah critically eyeing the slide as she went along. She led off on the way down, and it was no slight test of activity to do so. The hill was steep, the causeway often interrupted, and the ground rough. The only way to avoid being thrown down by such obstacles was to regain the perpendicular by a desperate leap forwards, or to take a run when they could not slide, and so running, leaping, flying, to make their way to the bottom. Again and again they tramped up the hill, and flew down, each time leaping into the snow-drift at the bottom till all were assembled. They were laying in a stock of courage, health, and energy that would benefit them for the whole of their natural lives. True, they were most of them forbidden to do it, but they were blessed with a healthy instinct that set authority at defiance.

BRANWELL BRONTË
(1817–1848)

Branwell Brontë was the only boy of the six Brontë children. He often felt overshadowed by his more talented and successful sisters, Emily, Anne and Charlotte. In 1838 he set himself up as a portrait painter, but the venture proved unsuccessful. There followed a variety of jobs, most of which ended badly. The poem here reflects something of the mental torment he suffered through much of his life.

On Peaceful Death and Painful Life

Why dost thou sorrow for the happy dead?
For if their life be lost, their toils are o'er
And woe and want shall trouble them no more,
Nor ever slept they in an earthly bed
So sound as now they sleep while, dreamless, laid
In the dark chambers of that unknown shore
Where Night and Silence seal each guarded door:
So, turn from such as these thy drooping head
And mourn the "Dead alive" whose spirit flies—
Whose life departs before his death has come—
Who finds no Heaven beyond Life's gloomy skies
Who sees no Hope to brighten up that gloom,
'Tis HE who feels the worm that never dies—
The REAL death and darkness of the tomb.

CHARLOTTE BRONTË
(1816–1855)

Stung by the critics' reception to *Jane Eyre*, Charlotte Brontë set out to create 'something real and severe and unromantic as Monday morning'. The resulting novel was written under unimaginably distressing circumstances, as Charlotte had lost her three siblings in less than a year. In *Shirley*, Charlotte does not master the 'social novel' as well as Dickens, or her contemporaries Elizabeth Gaskell and George Eliot. She was on much more comfortable ground when she returned to the world of women's education and relationships in her final novel, *Villette* (1853).

Shirley is set in the Spen Valley area of Yorkshire at the time of the Luddite riots, a period her father had experienced as a curate in the area. Charlotte based some of the characters on her friends, the Taylor family of Red House, and she used nearby Oakwell Hall in West Yorkshire, now a museum, as the basis for her descriptions of Fieldhead in the novel. This extract describes the attack on Hollow's Mill.

from Shirley

"What are they doing now, Shirley? What is that noise?"

"Hatchets and crow-bars against the yard-gates: they are forcing them. Are you afraid?"

"No; but my heart throbs fast; I have a difficulty in standing: I will sit down. Do you feel unmoved?"

"Hardly that—but I am glad I came: we shall see what transpires with our own eyes: we are here on the spot, and none know it. Instead of amazing the curate, the clothier, and the corn-dealer with a romantic rush on the stage, we stand alone with the friendly night, its mute stars, and these whispering trees, whose report our friends will not come to gather."

"Shirley—Shirley, the gates are down! That crash was like the felling of great trees. Now they are pouring through. They will break down the mill-doors as they have broken the gates: what can Robert do against so many? Would to God I were a little nearer him—could hear him speak—could speak to him! With my will—my longing to serve him—I could not be a useless burden in his way: I could be turned to some account."

"They come on!" cried Shirley. "How steadily they march in! There is discipline in their ranks—I will not say there is courage: hundreds against tens are no proof of that quality; but" (she dropped her voice) "there is suffering and desperation enough amongst them—these goads will urge them forwards."

"Forwards against Robert—and they hate him. Shirley, is there much danger they will win the day?"

"We shall see. Moore and Helstone are of 'earth's first blood'—no bunglers—no cravens——"

A crash—smash—shiver—stopped their whispers. A simultaneously-hurled volley of stones had saluted the broad front of the mill, with all its windows; and now every pane of every lattice lay in shattered and pounded fragments. A yell followed this demonstration—a rioters' yell—a North-of-England—a Yorkshire—a West-Riding— a West-Riding-clothing-district-of-Yorkshire rioters' yell. You never heard that sound, perhaps, reader? So much the better for your ears—perhaps for your heart; since, if it rends the air in hate to yourself, or to the men or principles you approve, the interests to which you wish well, Wrath wakens to the cry of Hate: the Lion shakes his mane, and rises to the howl of the Hyæna: Caste stands up, ireful, against Caste; and the indignant, wronged spirit of the Middle Rank bears down in zeal and scorn on the famished and furious mass of the Operative Class. It is difficult to be tolerant—difficult to be just—in such moments.

Caroline rose; Shirley put her arm round her: they stood together as still as the straight stems of two trees. That yell was a long one, and when it ceased, the night was yet full of the swaying and murmuring of a crowd.

"What next?" was the question of the listeners. Nothing came yet. The mill remained mute as a mausoleum.

"He *cannot* be alone!" whispered Caroline.

"I would stake all I have, that he is as little alone as he is alarmed," responded Shirley.

Shots were discharged by the rioters. Had the defenders waited for this signal? It seemed so. The hitherto inert and passive mill woke: fire flashed from its empty window-frames; a volley of musketry pealed sharp through the Hollow.

"Moore speaks at last!" said Shirley, "and he seems to have the gift of tongues; that was not a single voice."

"He has been for bearing; no one can accuse him of rashness," alleged Caroline: "their discharge preceded his; they broke his gates and his windows; they fired at his garrison before he repelled them."

What was going on now? It seemed difficult, in the darkness, to distinguish, but something terrible, a still-renewing tumult, was obvious: fierce attacks, desperate repulses; the mill-yard, the mill itself, was full of battle-movement: there was scarcely any cessation now of the discharge of firearms; and there was struggling, rushing, trampling, and shouting between. The aim of the assailants seemed to be to enter the mill, that of the defendants to beat them off. They heard the rebel leader cry, "To the back, lads!" They heard a voice retort, "Come round, we will meet you!"

"To the counting-house!" was the order again.

"Welcome!—We shall have you there!" was the response. And accordingly, the fiercest blaze that had yet glowed, the loudest rattle that had yet been heard, burst from the counting-house front, when the mass of rioters rushed up to it.

The voice that had spoken was Moore's own voice. They could tell by its tones that his soul was now warm with the conflict: they could guess that the fighting animal was roused in every one of those men there struggling together, and was for the time quite paramount above the rational human being. Both the girls felt their faces glow and their pulses throb: both knew they would do no good by rushing down into the mêlée: they desired neither to deal nor to receive blows; but they could not have run away—Caroline no more than Shirley; they could not have fainted; they could not have taken their eyes from the dim, terrible scene—from the mass of cloud, of smoke—the musket-lightning—for the world.

"How and when would it end?" was the demand throbbing in their throbbing pulses. "Would a juncture arise in which they could be useful?" was what they waited to see; for, though Shirley put off their too-late arrival with a jest, and was ever ready to satirize her own or any other person's enthusiasm, she would have given a farm of her best land for a chance of rendering good service.

The chance was not vouchsafed her; the looked-for juncture never came: it was not likely. Moore had expected this attack for days, perhaps weeks: he was prepared for it at every point. He had fortified and garrisoned his mill, which in itself was a strong building: he was a cool, brave man: he stood to the defence with unflinching firmness; those who were with him caught his spirit, and copied his demeanour. The rioters had never been so met before. At other mills they had attacked, they had found no resistance; an organized, resolute defence was what they never dreamed of encountering. When their leaders saw the steady fire kept up from the mill, witnessed the composure and determination of its owner, heard themselves coolly defied and invited on to death, and beheld their men falling wounded round them, they felt that nothing was to be done here. In haste, they mustered their forces, drew them away from the building: a roll was called over, in which the men answered to figures instead of names: they dispersed wide over the fields, leaving silence and ruin behind them. The attack, from its commencement to its termination, had not occupied an hour.

Day was by this time approaching: the west was dim, the east beginning to gleam. It would have seemed that the girls who had watched this conflict would now wish to hasten to the victors, on whose side all their interest had been enlisted; but they only very cautiously approached the now battered mill, and, when suddenly a number of soldiers and gentlemen appeared at the great door opening into the yard, they quickly stepped aside into a shed, the deposit of old iron and timber, whence they could see without being seen.

It was no cheering spectacle: these premises were now a mere blot of desolation on the fresh front of the summer-dawn. All the copse up the Hollow was shady and dewy, the hill at its head was green; but just here in the centre of the sweet glen, Discord, broken loose in the night from control, had beaten the ground with his stamping hoofs, and left it waste and pulverized. The mill yawned all ruinous with unglazed frames; the yard was thickly bestrewn with stones and brickbats, and, close under the mill, with the glittering fragments of the shattered windows; muskets and other weapons lay here and there; more than one deep crimson stain was visible on the gravel: a human body lay quiet on its face near the gates; and five or six wounded men writhed and moaned in the bloody dust.

DAVID STUART DAVIES

'The Cottingley Fairies'

Arthur Conan Doyle, creator of Sherlock Holmes, and
respected public figure, became a great advocate of
Spiritualism following the First World War in which his
son Kingsley and brother Innes both lost their lives. The
deaths caused him to seek answers for the cruelty of
such occurrences and led to his growing acceptance of
claims by mediums and clairvoyants that death was not
the end and there was a spiritual world which could be
contacted. This firm belief allowed Doyle to be fooled
by two Yorkshire girls who claimed to have photographed fairies in their garden in Cottingley, a village
nestling in the countryside between Bingley and Bradford.

It was in 1917 that cousins Elsie and Frances Wright
used Elsie's father's camera to photograph fairies and
elves flitting round a stream near their home. They
claimed that these ethereal creatures were their frequent
playmates. The photographs and accounts of the inci-
dents were published in 1920 and a great deal of
controversy ensued. Doyle reviewed the case carefully.
He showed the photographs to his Spiritualist friends
including Sir Oliver Lodge, who dismissed them as
fakes. Conan Doyle refused to accept that two young
girls could be so devious and accomplished as to create

these images. Determined to discover the truth, the author took the photographs to the London offices of Kodak in Kingsway. Their experts could find no proof of the superimposition of the fairy images, but they did admit that it was possible for them to reproduce such photographs themselves if required. This was not what Doyle wanted to hear so he ignored their findings.

In July 1920 Edward L. Gardner, a Theosophist colleague of Doyle and a believer in the existence of fairies, visited Cottingley to meet the girls. They showed him the camera they had used and produced another set of photographs. When Doyle saw them, he was delighted and wrote to Gardner: 'When fairies are admitted other psychic phenomena will find a more easy acceptance.'

The second set of prints confirmed to the gullible Doyle that they were a genuine confirmation of the spirit world made manifest, and it was his duty to inform the world of their significance. The truth is that he wanted to believe in them; he wanted to believe that fairies lived in dells by streams in Yorkshire. He wrote a detailed account of the affair, which was published in the Christmas 1920 edition of the *Strand Magazine*. To protect the girls' privacy he used pseudonyms, but the press soon uncovered the truth and he was scorned by the tabloids and pilloried by the broadsheets for his credulity. It was not long before he became the butt of jokes, but the author remained adamant in his beliefs and in 1922 went on to write a book, *The Coming of the Fairies*. In this much derided volume he wrote:

'I have convinced myself that there is overwhelming

evidence for fairies . . . We see objects within the limits which make up how our colour spectrum, with infinite vibrations, unused by us, on either side of them. If we could conceive a race of beings which were constructed in material which threw out shorter or longer vibrations, they would be invisible unless we could tune ourselves up or tone them down. It is exactly that power of tuning up and adapting itself to other vibrations which constitutes a clairvoyant, and there is nothing scientifically impossible, so far as I can see, in some people seeing that which is invisible to others. If the objects are indeed there, and if the inventive power of the human brain is turned upon the problem, it is likely that some sort of psychic spectacles, inconceivable to us at the moment, will be invented, and that we shall all be able to adapt ourselves to the new conditions. If high tension electricity can be converted by a mechanical contrivance into lower tension, keyed to other uses, then it is hard to see why something analogous might not with the vibrations of ether and the waves of light.'

Such gobbledygook clearly demonstrates that Doyle's determination to believe in the fairy world had muddled his thinking and blinded him to the obvious. For the man who created the sharp-witted detective Sherlock Holmes, Doyle was particularly dim in the Cottingley affair. He dismissed as insignificant the fact that Elsie Wright worked several months for a photographer because he did not feel she could have acquired the knowledge necessary to fake a photographic plate. He believed that the procedure was technically complicated

and something a teenager could not possibly understand. Nevertheless, one would have thought that Elsie's
involvement with a photographer's studio should have
raised some suspicion in the author's mind – but apparently not.

It is true however that the fairy photographs were not
created by technical means or the manipulation of
plates and prints. They were created more simply by
using cardboard two-dimensional drawings of fairies
and three-dimensional fairy dolls. In 1983 Elsie Wright
gave a television interview in which she admitted that
the photographs were faked, saying she and her cousin
had attached paper cutouts to the bushes with hairpins
and then photographed each other with their fairy crea-
tions. At the time of the publication of the photographs,
critics pointed out that some of the fairies were identi-
cal to those seen in printed advertisements for a
particular magazine. It is very hard to explain why
Doyle could have been taken in completely by these
rather crude photographs which were concocted by two
clever Yorkshire lasses. It certainly was a low point in the
author's distinguished career.

ANNE LISTER
(1791–1840)

Anne Lister was from a landowning family at Shibden Hall, near Halifax, which is now a museum. She was bold, fiercely independent and a lesbian, conducting multiple affairs from her schooldays onwards, often while travelling abroad. She dressed in black, disregarding conventional female dress and was later known as 'Gentleman Jack'. Her final significant partner was Ann Walker, to whom she was notionally married in Holy Trinity Church, Goodramgate, York, which is now celebrated as the birthplace of lesbian marriage. She kept intimate diaries of her life and loves, much of which was written in code. They reveal a great deal about contemporary life in Yorkshire and her remarkable frank description of her romantic liaisons. Here are extracts from her diaries describing Christmases in Halifax and York.

from The Diaries of Anne Lister

HALIFAX, THURSDAY, 25TH DECEMBER 1817

We all went to morning church and stayed the sacrament. Assisted my aunt in reading prayers in the afternoon. In the evening, read aloud sermons 8 and 9, Hoole. A remarkably fine, frosty day. Roads very slippery. Barometer 1½ deg. above changeable. Fahr. 29° at 9 p.m.

HALIFAX, FRIDAY, 26TH DECEMBER 1817

Went without dinner today, not having felt well since I came home (bilious and heavy) which I solely attribute to dining at 3 p.m. and which certainly never agrees with me. Went downstairs to dessert and then walked to meet 'M' on her way from York to Lawton, through Leeds by Burstall, and met her (and the cook, Elizabeth, she had hired in York) in the landau a few yards beyond the Hipperholme bar. I was pleased to find she had very good horses and very civil drivers from the Rose & Crown (Leeds) and which were in readiness according to my orders at one, exactly the time she reached Leeds. 'M' arrived here at five by the kitchen clock, three-quarters past four by the Halifax, and quarter-past four by Leeds and York. She brought me a small parcel from Nantz, containing a very kind note from herself and one from Lou, and a pair of cambric muslin sleeves with broad wrist bands to be worn as linings, which she (Nantz) had made, and another pair which she had altered for me. After tea, 'M' and I played whist against my uncle and aunt and won a rubber of four and a game. Very fine, frosty day.

Came upstairs twenty minutes before eleven, but sat up talking till twelve. After all, I believe 'M's' heart is all my own. 'M' told us, after tea, what a narrow escape Mr C— L— had just had the other day of being shot. In getting over a hedge, something caught the trigger, the gun went off and the contents only just missed. A similar accident, I understand, occurred to him just before 'M' and Louisa left Lawton, and his glove and waistcoat were a good deal burnt.

HALIFAX, 25TH DECEMBER 1818

We all walked to morning church. Mr West of South-owram preached. Afterwards wished us 'A merry Christmas'. All stayed the sacrament. I fear I never received it with less feeling of reverence. Was thinking more of Miss Browne than anything else. She was there opposite me at the altar table.

HALIFAX, 26TH DECEMBER 1818

Went down the north parade and sat half an hour at Cross-hills. The whole kit of them at home and vulgar as ever. Miss Caroline's head like a porcupine. Surely Mrs Greenwood must drink . . . During supper, fired the pistols.

HALIFAX, 28TH DECEMBER 1818

My aunt and I set off to Halifax at half-past two, she having, just before, gathered out of the garden for my Aunt Lister, a nosegay of fifteen different sorts of flowers – laurustinus, chrysanthemums, yellow jasmine, pink-tree flower, dwarf passion-flower, heart's ease, double primrose, purple stock, auricula, sweet allison, Venus's looking-glass, gentianella, roses, larkspur, and pheasant's eye – and three or four more sorts might have been added, such has been this uncommon season.

HALIFAX, FRIDAY, 31ST DECEMBER 1819

In the afternoon . . . to the Saltmarshes'. Stayed rather above an hour and got home at 5.10. Better satisfied with my visit than usual. Thought them glad enough to see me and I said nothing I wished unsaid. From Emma's account, their ball must have been a riotous concern. The Greenwoods and Miss Mary Haigue dance riotously and Tom Rawson took Mrs Prescott and danced her on his knee before them all, having before as publicly tickled her daughter, Elizabeth, on the sofa. She and Miss Mary Haigue afterwards went into another room. Tom kissed them both. Emma was obliged to leave them and Mr Saltmarshe and Mrs Walker of Crow Nest unluckily went in together and caught them. He had his arm round Mary Haigue's neck, but she looked nothing abashed. Mrs Christopher Rawson took Miss Astley with her, the Unitarian Minister's sister. Tom said, 'It is a long time since I have had a kiss of you.' Mr Christopher gave her one, said the ladies will think it rude if it does not go round, and though he had never seen Miss Astley before, put his arm round her neck and kissed her also.

A good deal of snow fell last night and the morning was snowy till after ten.

FRIDAY, 21ST DECEMBER 1821, AT YORK

The mare stiffish and rather knocked up with her journey yesterday, and I could not get off from Low Grange till eleven. Drove off in the midst of wind and rain which were just come on. Tried the mare with a pint of warm ale at Simpson's but she would not touch, nor did she eat well this morning or yesterday. Never saw an animal so idle and sluggish withal. She took more whipping even than yesterday and, a little beyond Barby Moor new inn, seemed determined to go no further. Went back to the house to get a poster. The man at the inn said it would break a pair. His horses were much worked by the coaches, etc., and civilly but positively said he really could not let me have a horse. Gave the mare a little warm water and made George drive forwards to York. The mare stopped two or three times and would turn in at two or three public houses by the way, and by dint of hard whipping brought us here at last (Dr Belcombe's, Petergate) in four hours . . . So sleepy with being so much out in the air, and so harassed one way or other that I could scarce keep my eyes open and was obliged to come upstairs to bed directly after tea.

'M' and I went to speak to Mrs Small in College Street, who keeps the most respectable register office for servants in York. We then went to the Minster in time for the anthem, and walked about the aisles till service was over. What a magnificent building. How striking the effect of its being lighted up throughout! Which it is every Sunday, and was today . . .

After dinner, all danced and made merry with the children, and I, while they played with them, came upstairs and finished the journal of yesterday and wrote this of today.

EMILY BRONTË
(1818–1848)

Emily Brontë's poetry is amongst the most highly regarded in the English language. Of all the Brontës she was the most influenced by the wild moorland scenery around her home at Haworth. Only a handful of Emily's personal papers and manuscripts have survived and so she and the meaning of her work remain an enigma to readers and biographers alike.

Winter Storms

Wild the road and rough and dreary;
Barren all the moorland round;
Rude the couch that rests us weary;
Mossy stone and heathy ground.

But, when winter storms were meeting
In the moonless, midnight dome,
Did we heed the tempest's beating,
Howling round our spirits' home?

No; that tree with branches riven,
Whitening in the whirl of snow,
As it tossed against the heaven,
Sheltered happy hearts below –

The Night is Darkening Round Me

The night is darkening round me,
The wild winds coldly blow;
But a tyrant spell has bound me,
And I cannot, cannot go.

The giant trees are bending
Their bare boughs weighed with snow;
The storm is fast descending,
And yet I cannot go.

Clouds beyond clouds above me,
Wastes beyond wastes below;
But nothing drear can move me;
I will not, cannot go.

Elizabeth Gaskell
(1810–1865)

Elizabeth Gaskell was fascinated by the author of *Jane Eyre*. By the time the two women met she had already formed a romantic notion of her life in Haworth and, after Charlotte's death, when it was agreed that she would write her biography, she used her novelist's eye in penning her story. This extract recounts Gaskell's visit to Haworth. It is thanks to Elizabeth Gaskell that first-hand impressions of the Brontë family are preserved but she also continued what the Brontës themselves, by adopting pseudonyms, had unwittingly begun: the growing myth of the Brontës of Haworth, which developed a life of its own.

from The Life of Charlotte Brontë

Towards the latter end of September I went to Haworth. At the risk of repeating something which I have previously said, I will copy out parts of a letter which I wrote at the time.

'It was a dull, drizzly Indian-inky day, all the way on the railroad to Keighley, which is a rising wool-manufacturing town, lying in a hollow between hills—not a pretty hollow, but more what the Yorkshire people call a "bottom," or "botham." I left Keighley in a car for Haworth, four miles off—four tough, steep, scrambling miles, the road winding between the wave-like hills that rose and fell on every side of the horizon, with a long illimitable sinuous look, as if they were a part of the line of the Great Serpent, which the Norse legend says girdles the world. The day was lead-coloured; the road had stone factories alongside of it,—grey, dull-coloured rows of stone cottages belonging to these factories, and then we came to poor, hungry-looking fields;—stone fences everywhere, and trees nowhere. Haworth is a long, straggling village: one steep narrow street—so steep that the flag-stones with which it is paved are placed end-ways, that the horses' feet may have something to cling to, and not slip down backwards; which if they did, they would soon reach Keighley. But if the horses had cats' feet and claws, they would do all the better. Well, we (the man, horse, car, and I) clambered up this street, and reached the church dedicated to St Autest (who was he?); then we turned off into a lane on the left, past the curate's lodging at the Sexton's, past the school-house, up to the Parsonage yard-door. I went round the house to the front door, looking to the church;—moors everywhere beyond and above. The crowded grave-yard surrounds the house and small grass enclosure for drying clothes.

'I don't know that I ever saw a spot more exquisitely clean; the most dainty place for that I ever saw. To be sure, the life is like clock-work. No one comes to the house; nothing disturbs the deep repose; hardly a voice is heard; you catch the ticking of the clock in the kitchen, or the buzzing of a fly in the parlour, all over the house. Miss Brontë sits alone in her parlour; breakfasting with her father in his study at nine o'clock. She helps in the housework; for one of their servants, Tabby, is nearly ninety, and the other only a girl. Then I accompanied her in her walks on the sweeping moors: the heather-bloom had been blighted by a thunder-storm a day or two before, and was all of a livid brown colour, instead of the blaze of purple glory it ought to have been. Oh! those high, wild, desolate moors, up above the whole world, and the very realms of silence! Home to dinner at two. Mr Brontë has his dinner sent into him. All the small table arrangements had the same dainty simplicity about them. Then we rested, and talked over the clear, bright fire; it is a cold country, and the fires were a pretty warm dancing light all over the house. The parlour has been evidently refurnished within the last few years, since Miss Brontë's success has enabled her to have a little more money to spend. Everything fits into, and is in harmony with, the idea of a country parsonage, possessed by people of very moderate means. The prevailing colour of the room is crimson, to make a warm setting for the cold grey landscape without. There is her likeness by Richmond, and an engraving from Lawrence's picture of Thackeray; and two recesses, on each side of the high, narrow, old-fashioned mantel-piece, filled with books,—books given to her, books she has bought, and which tell of her individual pursuits and tastes; *not* standard books.

'She cannot see well, and does little beside knitting. The way she weakened her eyesight was this: when she was sixteen or seventeen, she wanted much to draw; and she copied nimini-pimini copper-plate engravings out of annuals, ("stippling," don't the artists call it?) every little point put in, till at the end of six months she had produced an exquisitely faithful copy of the engraving. She wanted to learn to express her ideas by drawing. After she had tried to *draw* stories, and not succeeded, she took the better mode of writing; but in so small a hand, that it is almost impossible to decipher what she wrote at this time.

'But now to return to our quiet hour of rest after dinner. I soon observed that her habits of order were such that she could not go on with the conversation, if a chair was out of its place; everything was arranged with delicate regularity. We talked over the old times of her childhood; of her elder sister's (Maria's) death,—just like that of Helen Burns in "Jane Eyre;" of the desire (almost amounting to illness) of expressing herself in some way,—writing or drawing; of her weakened eyesight, which prevented her doing anything for two years, from the age of seventeen to nineteen; of her being a governess; of her going to Brussels; whereupon I said I disliked Lucy Snowe, and we discussed M. Paul Emanuel; and I told her of ——'s admiration of "Shirley," which pleased her for the character of Shirley was meant for her sister Emily, about whom she is never tired of talking, nor I of listening. Emily must have been a remnant of the Titans,—great-grand-daughter of the giants who used to inhabit earth. One day, Miss Brontë brought down a rough, common-looking oil-painting, done by her brother, of herself,—a little, rather prim-looking girl of eighteen,—and the two other sisters, girls of sixteen and fourteen, with cropped hair, and sad, dreamy-looking eyes. . . . Emily had a great dog,—half mastiff, half bull-dog—so savage, &c. . . . This dog went to her funeral, walking side by side with her father; and then, to the day of its death, it slept at her room door, snuffing under it, and whining every morning.

'We have generally had another walk before tea, which is at six; at half-past eight, prayers; and by nine, all the household are in bed, except ourselves. We sit up together till ten, or past; and after I go, I hear Miss Brontë come down and walk up and down the room for an hour or so.'

ANNE BRONTË
(1820–1849)

Anne Brontë's second novel, *The Tenant of Wildfell Hall*, is one of the most remarkable in English literature, exposing the abuse suffered by women at the hands of men. Its shocking depictions of violence and the deterioration of someone experiencing an alcohol problem were too much for the critics of the time, although the novel was a commercial success. Charlotte, to protect her sisters' reputations, and her own family's, suppressed its publication after Anne's death. In this scene, Helen faces her abusive husband Arthur Huntingdon, who destroys her art materials, emphasizing the power that men had over their wives. In the nineteenth century, women lost all rights to their property on marriage and Helen Huntingdon takes the bold step of leaving her husband, creating mystery and scandal when she moves to Wildfell Hall to a new life. Set in an unidentified part of the north of England, the isolated house in a dramatic landscape shares features with Emily's Wuthering Heights.

from The Tenant of Wildfell Hall

January 10th, 1827. While writing the above, yesterday evening, I sat in the drawing-room. Mr Huntingdon was present, but, as I thought, asleep on the sofa behind me. He had risen however, unknown to me, and, actuated by some base spirit of curiosity, been looking over my shoulder for I know not how long; for when I had laid aside my pen, and was about to close the book, he suddenly placed his hand upon it, and saying – 'With your leave, my dear, I'll have a look at this,' forcibly wrested it from me, and, drawing a chair to the table, composedly sat down to examine it – turning back leaf after leaf to find an explanation of what he had read. Unluckily for me, he was more sober that night than he usually is at such an hour.

Of course I did not leave him to pursue this occupation in quiet: I made several attempts to snatch the book from his hands, but he held it too firmly for that; I upbraided him in bitterness and scorn for his mean and dishonourable conduct, but that had no effect upon him; I extinguished both the candles, but he only wheeled round to the fire, and raising a blaze sufficient for his purposes, calmly continued the investigation. I had serious thoughts of getting a pitcher of water and extinguishing that light too; but it was evident his curiosity was too keenly excited to be quenched by that, and the more I manifested my anxiety to baffle his scrutiny, the greater would be his determination to persist in it – besides it was too late.

'It seems very interesting, love,' said he, lifting his head and turning to where I stood wringing my hands in silent rage and anguish; 'but it's rather long; I'll look at it some other time; and meanwhile, I'll trouble you for your keys, my dear.'

'What keys?'

'The keys of your cabinet, desk, drawers, and whatever else you possess,' said he, rising and holding out his hand.

'I've not got them,' I replied. The key of my desk, in fact, was, at that moment, in the lock, and the others were attached to it.

'Then you must send for them,' said he; 'and if that old bitch, Rachel, doesn't immediately deliver them up, she tramps bag and baggage tomorrow.'

'She doesn't know where they are,' I answered, quietly placing my hand upon them, and taking them from the desk, as I thought, unobserved. '*I* know, but I shall not give them up without a reason.'

'And *I* know, too,' said he, suddenly seizing my closed hand and rudely abstracting them from it. He then took up one of the candles and relighted it by thrusting it into the fire.

'Now then,' sneered he, 'we must have a confiscation of property. But first, let us take a peep into the studio.' And putting the keys into his pocket, he walked into the library. I followed, whether with the dim idea of preventing mischief or only to know the worst I can hardly tell.

My painting materials were laid together on the corner table, ready for tomorrow's use, and only covered with a cloth. He soon spied them out, and putting down the candle, deliberately proceeded to cast them into the fire – palette, paints, bladders, pencils, brushes, varnish – I saw them all consumed – the palette knives snapped in two – the oil and turpentine sent hissing and roaring up the chimney. He then rang the bell.

'Benson, take those things away,' said he, pointing to the easel, canvass, and stretcher; 'and tell the house-maid she may kindle the fire with them: your mistress won't want them any more.'

Benson paused aghast and looked at me.

'Take them away, Benson,' said I; and his master muttered an oath.

'And this and all, sir?' said the astonished servant referring to the half-finished picture.

'That and all,' replied the master; and the things were cleared away.

Mr Huntingdon then went upstairs. I did not attempt to follow him, but remained seated in the arm-chair, speechless, tearless, and almost motionless, till he returned about half an hour after, and walking up to me, held the candle in my face and peered into my eyes with looks and laughter too insulting to be borne. With a sudden stroke of my hand, I dashed the candle to the floor.

ANDREW MARVELL
(1621–1678)

Perhaps Andrew Marvell's most famous work is the witty poem of seduction tinged with cynicism 'To His Coy Mistress'. It is a carpe diem poem which follows the example of the Roman poets like Horace. It is an attempt to seduce the titular 'coy mistress', urging her to enjoy the passionate pleasures of life before death overtakes her.

To His Coy Mistress

Had we but world enough, and time,
This coyness, lady, were no crime.
We would sit down, and think which way
To walk, and pass our long love's day.
Thou by the Indian Ganges' side
Should'st rubies find: I by the tide
Of Humber would complain. I would
Love you ten years before the Flood,
And you should, if you please, refuse
Till the conversion of the Jews.
My vegetable love should grow
Vaster than empires, and more slow
An hundred years should go to praise
Thine eyes, and on thy forehead gaze:
Two hundred to adore each breast;
But thirty thousand to the rest;
An age at least to every part,
And the last age should show your heart.
For, lady, you deserve this state,
Nor would I love at lower rate.

But at my back I always hear
Time's wingèd chariot hurrying near:
And yonder all before us lie
Deserts of vast eternity.
Thy beauty shall no more be found;

Nor, in thy marble vault, shall sound
My echoing song: then worms shall try
That long-preserved virginity,
And your quaint honour turn to dust,
And into ashes all my lust.
The grave's a fine and private place,
But none, I think, do there embrace.

Now, therefore, while the youthful hue
Sits on thy skin like morning dew,
And while thy willing soul transpires
At every pore with instant fires,
Now let us sport us while we may;
And now, like amorous birds of prey,
Rather at once our Time devour,
Than languish in his slow-chapt power.
Let us roll all our strength and all
Our sweetness up into one ball,
And tear our pleasures with rough strife
Thorough the iron gates of life.
Thus, though we cannot make our Sun
Stand still, yet we will make him run.

TOWNS AND CITIES

KEITH WATERHOUSE
(1929–2009)

Keith Waterhouse's wonderful creation Billy Liar was so successful that the character moved from novel to play to film to a musical stage show. To young Billy Fisher's mind no one really understands him. He is trapped in a mundane workaday world with little chance of excitement and recognition. So he spices up his existence through his untruths and fantasies in order to escape his humdrum life. He is, in essence, the Walter Mitty of Yorkshire. In this tragi-comic novel, published in 1959, Waterhouse, born in Hunslet near Leeds, captures the dull minutiae of life in a small Yorkshire town, the fictional Stradhoughton, in the 1950s. Billy longs to leave the town and head for the bright lights of London to be a script writer – he tells people that is what he is going to do, but he lacks the courage to do it. The real unknown is too frightening for him and in the end he retreats into the safety of daydreams.

from Billy Liar

Councillor Duxbury came flapping down the stone path, raising his stick in salute.

'Afternoon, lad!' he called in his rich, so-called York-shire relish voice.

'Afternoon, Councillor!' I called in the robust voice.

'It's a sunny 'un, this! 'Appen tha's watching t' foot-ball?'

'Nay, ahm' just bahn for a walk ower t' moor.' I always talked to Councillor Duxbury in his own dialect, half-mockingly, half-compulsively, usually goading myself into internal hysterics when I thought how I would reproduce the conversation to Arthur later.

'What's ta got theer, then? T' crown jewels?' He pointed with his stick at my parcel, his old face set in the serious, deadpan expression that had won him his tiresome reputation as a wag in the council chamber.

'Nay, old gramophone records,' I said, wildly pro-ducing the one record I did have, as proof. He did not ask me where I was taking them.

'Aye, ther' were nowt like that,' he said. His memory had been jogged so many times by *Echo* interviews that he now regarded every statement as a cue for his reminiscences, and no longer bothered to add 'when I were a lad' or 'fot'ty year ago'. 'Ther' were nowt like that. We had to make our own music if we wanted it, else go without.' He rattled on as though he were himself an old gramophone that has just been kicked back into action. I was not sure that he knew who I was. Entirely lost in himself he began to mumble about the *Messiah* and I let him, full of frothy self-congratulation because I would be one up on Arthur when the next Duxbury routine came up.

'No, ther' were nowt like that.' He stopped at last to wipe his nose, making a ritual of it with a coloured handkerchief about the size of a bed-sheet. He paused between sniffs and shot me what he imagined to be a playful glance, the expression he always wore when he asked people how old they thought he was.

'Does ta think ah could climb down yon ashpit?'

'Nay, tha'd break thi neck, Councillor!' I said, giving him entirely the wrong answer. He gave me a sour look and said: 'Aye, well ah'sll have to manage it, whether or no. Ah'm bahn down to t' police station.'

My heart missed another beat, or rather ceased operating altogether for a second.

'What's ta bahn down theer for, then?' I told myself optimistically that if it were about me he would be going to the town hall, never mind the local police station. Besides, he didn't know who I was.

Councillor Duxbury chuckled. 'We're pulling t' bugger down.'

I gulped with relief, although my heart was still at it. 'Tha's not, is ta?' I said, packing some incredulity into my voice.

'Aye, we are that. All yon cottages anall, they're

going. And they won't get *council* houses for three and six a week, neether.'

I shook my head in sympathy, and saw that he was going into another of his reveries. I transferred my parcel from one arm to the other.

'It's all change,' said Councillor Duxbury. 'All change, nowadays. T' old buildings is going. T' old street is going. T' trams, they've gone.'

'Aye,' I said, sighing with him. 'It's not t' same wi' t' buses, is it?' One good shove, I thought, and he would be down at the bottom of the ashpit, where he wanted to be.

'It were all horse-drawn trams, and afore that we had to walk. It's all change. T' old mills is going. T' old dialect, *that's* going,' he said. I suddenly realized that he knew perfectly well that I did not talk in dialect all the time, and also that it was ridiculous to imagine that he did not know I worked for him. To prevent him saying whatever he might have been going to say next, I began to talk, looking desperately down over Stradhoughton Moor.

'Well, progress is all very well,' I said. 'But it's a pity we don't have a Yorkshire tradition o' progress.' I was trying to modify the dialect so that I could drop out of it completely within the minute. I nodded down at the police station. 'I don't mind dark satanic mills, but by gum when it comes to dark satanic shops, dark satanic housing estates, and dark satanic police stations –' I broke off, realizing that I had never worked out the end of this sentence. I looked at Councillor Duxbury for the feedline but he was away, staring glassily over the Moor.

'– that's different,' I concluded lamely. He did not seem inclined to speak. 'And yet,' I went on, grabbing half-remembered tufts of my Man o' the Dales conversation, 'and yet we've got to remember, this isn't a religion, it's a county. We've, er –'

I tailed off again. Councillor Duxbury had the fixed expression that old men have when they are lost in their thoughts, or what they claim are their thoughts, not listening to a word I was saying. A quick gust of wind swept around our ankles. I opened my mouth to speak again, remembering another bit, and then suddenly, without moving, he carved straight into my monologue.

'Tha's a reet one wi' them calendars, i'n't ta?'

I blanched, rocked on my heels and nearly fell over the grass edge into the ashpit below. I looked into his face to see if there was any suspicion of a boys-will-be-boys chuckle, but he maintained his deadpan look as though he were telling wry jokes at a masonic dinner.

'By, that's capped me theer, Councillor!' was all I could think of to say.

'Aye, and tha's capped me anall! Ah were reet taken back when Shadrack rang me upon t' telephone. Ah'd ha' thowt a lad like thee would have had more sense.' He spoke easily and not sternly, like a Yorkshire butler filling in plot-lines in a dialect comedy. I fancied that he was peering with keen suspicion at the parcel of calendars, and wondered if it were true that there were wise old men and he was one of them. I didn't know what to make of it. Even if he knew I worked for him, I was surprised that he could distinguish me from Stamp and

Arthur. I had a reckless impulse to tell him that I *was* Arthur and that he was getting the two of us mixed up.

I said nothing.

'So tha's going to London, is ta?' he said with mild interest, as though the subject of the calendars had been settled entirely to his satisfaction.

Hopefully, I said: 'Aye, ah'm just about thraiped wi' Stradhoughton.' I remembered too late that 'thraiped' was a word Arthur and I had made up.

'How does ta mean?'

'It's neither muckling nor mickling,' I said, using another invented phrase in my complete panic.

'Aye.' The old man poked the ground with his stick, and said again, 'Aye.' I had no indication what he was thinking about at all. I tried hard to keep talking, but I could not think of a single word of any description.

'Well tha's gotten me in a very difficult position,' he said weightily, at last.

'How does ta mean, Councillor?'

He studied me keenly, and I realized for the first time, with a sinking heart, that he was not as daft as he looked.

'Is ta taking a rise out o' me, young man?'

I felt myself flushing, and found my whole personality shifting into the familiar position of sheepishness and guilt. 'No, of course not.'

'Well just talk as thi mother and father brought thee up to talk, then. Ah've had no education, ah had to educate myself, but that's no reason for thee to copy t' way *I* talk.' He spoke sharply but kindly, in a voice of authority with some kind of infinite wisdom behind it, and at that moment I felt genuinely ashamed.

'Now sither. We'll noan go ower t' ins and outs of it, tha's been ower all that down at t' office. But young Shadrack theer thinks ah ought to have a word wi' thi father about thee. What does ta say to that?'

'I don't know,' I muttered, hanging my head. I wondered how I could ask him, without actually begging for mercy, not to talk to the old man.

'Well don't look as if tha's lost a bob and fun sixpence! Tha's no deead yet!'

I looked up at him and gave him a thin, grateful smile.

'Straighten thi back up! That's better. Now sither. Ah don't know what ah'sll do. Ah'sll have to think about what's best. But sither –' He gripped my arm. I did not feel embarrassed; I was able, even, to look steadily into his eyes. 'Sither. Tha'rt a young man. Tha's got a long way to go. But tha can't do it by thisen. Now think on.'

He released my arm, leaving me feeling that he had said something sage and shrewd, although I was unable to fathom quite what he was getting at. He was stuffing his handkerchief into his overcoat pocket, preparing to go. I did not want him to go. I did not feel afraid. I felt a kind of tentative serenity and I wanted him to go on with his old man's advice, telling me the things I should do.

'My grandma's poorly,' I said suddenly, without even knowing that I was talking. But he did not seem to hear.

'Ah'm glad to have had t' chance o' talking to thee,' he said. He turned and began to make his way gingerly down the gentlest slope of the ashpit, feeling the way with his shiny stick. Half-way down he turned back awkwardly. 'Think on,' he said.

I looked down after him, only just beginning to realize that for the first time I wanted to tell somebody about it, and that I could very probably have explained it all to him. I had to resist an impulse to call back after him.

I stood there until he was safely on the grass perimeter surrounding the stretch of cinders. I had a feeling, one that I wanted to keep. It was a feeling of peace and melancholy. I was not at all afraid. I walked happily along the rough stone path through the allotments to the quiet moorland beyond, and even while I was burying the calendars the feeling was still with me.

BRAM STOKER
(1847–1912)

In this extract, Bram Stoker describes Whitby in attractive detail.

from Dracula

24 July, *Whitby* – Lucy met me at the station, looking sweeter and lovelier than ever, and we drove up to the house at the Crescent, in which they have rooms. This is a lovely place. The little river, the Esk, runs through a deep valley, which broadens out as it comes near the harbour. A great viaduct runs across, with high piers, through which the view seems, somehow, farther away than it really is. The valley is beautifully green, and it is so steep that when you are on the high land on either side you look right across it, unless you are near enough to see down. The houses of the old town – the side away from us – are all red-roofed, and seem piled up one over the other anyhow, like the pictures we see of Nuremberg. Right over the town is the ruin of Whitby Abbey, which was sacked by the Danes, and which is the scene of part of *Marmion*, where the girl was built up in the wall. It is a most noble ruin, of immense size, and full of beautiful and romantic bits; there is a legend that a white lady is seen in one of the windows. Between it and the town there is another church, the parish one, round which is a big graveyard, all full of tombstones. This is, to my mind, the nicest spot in Whitby, for it lies right over the town, and has a full view of the harbour and all up the bay to where the headland called Kettleness stretches out into the sea. It descends so steeply over

the harbour that part of the bank has fallen away, and some of the graves have been destroyed. In one place part of the stonework of the graves stretches out over the sandy pathway far below. There are walks, with seats beside them, through the churchyard; and people go and sit there all day long looking at the beautiful view and enjoying the breeze, I shall come and sit here very often myself and work.

ARTHUR H. NORWAY
(1859–1938)

Victorian historian Arthur H. Norway wrote several books about the various regions of Britain and in 1899 he produced *Highways & Byways in Yorkshire*, illustrated by the American artist Joseph Pennell and the Irish illustrator, Hugh Thomson. The book records Norway's journey through the Yorkshire countryside and his reflections on the places he visits and their heritage. His views on the city of York still have a remarkable relevance today.

from Highways and Byways in Yorkshire

But I really cannot stay to rake up these old scandals; for see, a turn of the road has brought in sight two noble towers standing side by side some three miles away, while at their base lies a crowd of buildings which can be no other than York. The first sight of that noble city drives out of my mind both erring nuns and their hotheaded lovers; and I hurry on my way scarce noting the pleasant houses of the suburb, or the green turf of the race-course, till I enter York itself beneath the massive arch of Micklegate, and stand in the narrow streets which still retain the aspect borne to them when the city was a fortress.

For York has never been modernised; our dull life has touched but not absorbed it. There are still the winding streets of ancient timbered houses nodding each towards the other, the old crumbling churches thrust out into the roadway and splitting it into two narrow lanes by which the traffic must filter onwards as it may. The small, quaint alleys winding to the river have not been improved away; the pleasant gardens here and there about the walls are as green and fresh as when the Stuart Kings or their wild courtiers jested there on summer evenings; the ancient gates and bars can still be closed when the rulers of the city will; and best of all, the traveller of to-day may walk around nearly the whole circuit of the walls and gaze forth still from the embrasures whence in the old days the warders looked for the smoke of beacons in the north, or watched some jaded rider spurring towards the city from Berwick to Carlisle.

These walls, once so formidable, are very quiet now; and you may pace up and down in solitude nearly all day long, while the sun flickers through the trees and gardens of the Deanery, while the swallows wheel and skim around the Minster towers, and the sound of chanting reaches you across the sweet, keen, northern air. You will walk onwards and note the great height which the walls have had. You will mark the towers and bastions which strengthened them; and going further you will see the blackened keep of the ancient castle standing by the river's bank, grim and strong, a clear witness even yet to the fact that those who fortified York anticipated no child's play, but feared assaults against which the best defences they could rear were not quite a whit so much. So, gradually, the modern peaceful aspect of the city falls away, and one sees York as it was, the ancient military centre of all England, the bulwark of the realm against the constant peril of the north.

CHARLES DICKENS
(1812–1870)

Charles Dickens was fond of Yorkshire, particularly Whitby, and visited the county several times. In 1838, he came to Yorkshire using a pseudonym to research Yorkshire boarding schools for his novel *Nicholas Nickleby*, then being serialized. These private boarding schools catered for the unwanted – often illegitimate children – of the rich. The youngsters were kept almost as prisoners throughout the year, at cheap rates. Dickens denounced the schools as examples of 'the monstrous neglect of Education in England'. These establishments were epitomized in the novel by Dotheboys Hall, run by the cruel and sadistic headmaster, Wackford Squeers. Dickens claimed that his depiction of Squeers and his school were 'faint and feeble pictures of an existing reality, purposely subdued and kept down lest they should be deemed impossible'. This formidable attack on such schools lent imaginative weight to indictments which had already been circulating, and helped to speed their demise.

from Nicholas Nickleby

OF THE INTERNAL ECONOMY OF DOTHEBOYS HALL

A ride of two hundred and odd miles in severe weather, is one of the best softeners of a hard bed that ingenuity can devise. Perhaps it is even a sweetener of dreams, for those which hovered over the rough couch of Nicholas, and whispered their airy nothings in his ear, were of an agreeable and happy kind. He was making his fortune very fast indeed, when the faint glimmer of an expiring candle shone before his eyes, and a voice he had no difficulty in recognising as part and parcel of Mr Squeers, admonished him that it was time to rise.

'Past seven, Nickleby,' said Mr Squeers.

'Has morning come already?' asked Nicholas, sitting up in bed.

'Ah! that has it,' replied Squeers, 'and ready iced too. Now, Nickleby, come; tumble up, will you?'

Nicholas needed no further admonition, but 'tumbled up' at once, and proceeded to dress himself by the light of the taper which Mr Squeers carried in his hand.

'Here's a pretty go,' said that gentleman; 'the pump's froze.'

'Indeed!' said Nicholas, not much interested in the intelligence.

'Yes,' replied Squeers. 'You can't wash yourself this morning.'

'Not wash myself!' exclaimed Nicholas.

'No, not a bit of it,' rejoined Squeers tartly. 'So you must be content with giving yourself a dry polish till we break the ice in the well, and can get a bucketful out for the boys. Don't stand staring at me, but do look sharp, will you?'

Offering no further observation, Nicholas huddled on his clothes, and Squeers meanwhile opened the shutters and blew the candle out, when the voice of his amiable consort was heard in the passage, demanding admittance.

'Come in, my love,' said Squeers.

Mrs Squeers came in, still habited in the primitive night-jacket which had displayed the symmetry of her figure on the previous night, and further ornamented with a beaver bonnet of some antiquity, which she wore with much ease and lightness upon the top of the night-cap before mentioned.

'Drat the things,' said the lady, opening the cupboard; 'I can't find the school spoon anywhere.'

'Never mind it, my dear,' observed Squeers in a soothing manner; 'it's of no consequence.'

'No consequence, why how you talk!' retorted Mrs Squeers sharply; 'isn't it brimstone morning?'

'I forgot, my dear,' rejoined Squeers; 'yes, it certainly is. We purify the boys' bloods now and then, Nickleby.'

'Purify fiddlesticks' ends,' said his lady. 'Don't think, young man, that we go to the expense of flower of brimstone and molasses just to purify them; because if you think we carry on the business in that way, you'll find yourself mistaken, and so I tell you plainly.'

'My dear,' said Squeers frowning. 'Hem!'

'Oh! nonsense,' rejoined Mrs Squeers. 'If the young man comes to be a teacher here, let him understand at once that we don't want any foolery about the boys. They have the brimstone and treacle, partly because if they hadn't something or other in the way of medicine they'd be always ailing and giving a world of trouble, and partly because it spoils their appetites and comes cheaper than breakfast and dinner. So it does them good and us good at the same time, and that's fair enough I'm sure.'

Having given this explanation, Mrs Squeers put her head into the closet and instituted a stricter search after the spoon, in which Mr Squeers assisted. A few words passed between them while they were thus engaged, but as their voices were partially stifled by the cupboard all that Nicholas could distinguish was, that Mr Squeers said what Mrs Squeers had said was injudicious, and that Mrs Squeers said what Mr Squeers said was 'stuff.'

A vast deal of searching and rummaging succeeded, and it proving fruitless, Smike was called in, and pushed by Mrs Squeers and boxed by Mr Squeers, which course of treatment brightening his intellects, enabled him to suggest that possibly Mrs Squeers might have the spoon in her pocket, as indeed turned out to be the case. As Mrs Squeers had previously protested, how-ever, that she was quite certain she had not got it, Smike received another box on the ear for presuming to con-tradict his mistress, together with a promise of a sound thrashing if he were not more respectful in future; so that he took nothing very advantageous by his motion.

'A most invaluable woman, that, Nickleby,' said Squeers when his consort had hurried away, pushing the drudge before her.

'Indeed, sir!' observed Nicholas.

'I don't know her equal,' said Squeers; 'I do not know her equal. That woman, Nickleby, is always the same – always the same bustling, lively, active, saving creetur that you see her now.'

Nicholas sighed involuntarily at the thought of the agreeable domestic prospect thus opened to him; but Squeers was, fortunately, too much occupied with his own reflections to perceive it.

'It's my way to say, when I am up in London,' continued Squeers, 'that to them boys she is a mother. But she is more than a mother to them, ten times more. She does things for them boys, Nickleby, that I don't believe half the mothers going would do for their own sons.'

'I should think they would not, sir,' answered Nicholas.

Now, the fact was, that both Mr and Mrs Squeers viewed the boys in the light of their proper and natural enemies; or, in other words, they held and considered that their business and profession was to get as much from every boy as could by possibility be screwed out of him. On this point they were both agreed, and behaved in unison accordingly. The only difference between them was, that Mrs Squeers waged war against the enemy openly and fearlessly, and that Squeers covered his rascality, even at home, with a spice of his habitual deceit, as if he really had a notion of some day or other being able to take himself in, and persuade his own mind that he was a very good fellow.

'But come,' said Squeers, interrupting the progress of some thoughts, to this effect in the mind of his usher, 'let's go to the school-room; and lend me a hand with my school-coat, will you?'

Nicholas assisted his master to put on an old fustian shooting-jacket, which he took down from a peg in the passage; and Squeers arming himself with his cane, led the way across a yard to a door in the rear of the house.

'There,' said the schoolmaster as they stepped in together; 'this is our shop, Nickleby.'

It was such a crowded scene, and there were so many objects to attract attention, that at first Nicholas stared about him, really without seeing anything at all. By degrees, however, the place resolved itself into a bare and dirty room with a couple of windows, whereof a tenth part might be of glass, the remainder being stopped up with old copy-books and paper. There were a couple of long old rickety desks, cut and notched, and inked and damaged, in every possible way; two or three forms, a detached desk for Squeers, and another for his assistant. The ceiling was supported like that of a barn, by cross beams and rafters, and the walls were so stained and discoloured, that it was impossible to tell whether they had ever been touched with paint or whitewash.

But the pupils – the young noblemen! How the last faint traces of hope, the remotest glimmering of any good to be derived from his efforts in this den, faded from the mind of Nicholas as he looked in dismay around! Pale and haggard faces, lank and bony figures, children with the countenances of old men, deformities with irons upon their limbs, boys of stunted growth, and others whose long meagre legs would hardly bear their stooping bodies, all crowded on the view together; there were the bleared eye, the hare-lip, the crooked foot, and every ugliness or distortion that told of unnatural aversion conceived by parents for their offspring, or of young lives which, from the earliest dawn of infancy, had been one horrible endurance of cruelty and neglect. There were little faces which should have been handsome, darkened with the scowl of sullen dogged suffering; there was childhood with the light of its eye quenched, its beauty gone, and its helplessness alone remaining; there were vicious-faced boys brooding, with leaden eyes, like malefactors in a jail; and there were young creatures on whom the sins of their frail parents had descended, weeping even for the mercenary nurses they had known, and lonesome even in their loneliness. With every kindly sympathy and affection blasted in its birth, with every young and healthy feeling flogged and starved down, with every revengeful passion that can fester in swollen hearts, eating its evil way to their core in silence, what an incipient Hell was breeding there!

And yet this scene, painful as it was, had its grotesque features, which, in a less interested observer than Nicholas, might have provoked a smile. Mrs Squeers stood at one of the desks, presiding over an immense basin of brimstone and treacle, of which delicious compound she administered a large instalment to each boy in succession, using for the purpose a common wooden spoon, which might have been originally manufactured for some gigantic top, and which widened every young gentleman's mouth considerably, they being all obliged, under heavy corporal penalties, to take in the whole of the bowl at a gasp. In another corner, huddled together for companionship, were the little boys who had arrived on the preceding night, three of them in very large leather breeches, and two in old trousers, a something tighter fit than drawers are usually worn; at no great distance from them was seated the juvenile son and heir of Mr Squeers – a striking likeness of his father – kicking with great vigour under the hands of Smike, who was fitting upon him a pair of new boots that bore a most suspicious resemblance to those which the least of the little boys had worn on the journey down, as the little boy himself seemed to think, for he was regarding the appropriation with a look of most rueful amazement. Besides these, there was a long row of boys waiting, with countenances of no pleasant anticipation, to be treacled, and another file who had just escaped from the infliction, making a variety of wry mouths indicative of anything but satisfaction. The whole were attired in such motley, ill-assorted, extraordinary garments, as would have been irresistibly ridiculous, but for the foul appearance of dirt, disorder, and disease, with which they were associated.

JOHN BRAINE
(1922–1986)

In the 1950s, when Britain was still recovering from the
ravages of the Second World War, there were several
novels set in the north of England which examined
working-class life and the rigid, stratified class system
that was prevalent at the time. Prominent amongst them
was *Room at the Top* (1957), written by John Braine. He
was born in Bradford but after the war moved to the
small town of Bingley where he wrote his groundbreaking novel. *Room at the Top* features Joe Lampton, an
ambitious, young working-class man who is desperate to
find room for himself at the top – in the higher echelons
of society, amongst the monied and powerful. He
believes that his best chance of climbing the social
ladder is to marry a rich man's daughter. He moves from
Dufton, the impoverished little town where he grew up,
to the big city of Leddesford (based on Bradford). In
this scene, Lampton returns to Dufton to visit his auntie
(his parents were killed in the war) and is struck by the
chasm that exists between his new life and the old.

from Room at the Top

We'd reached the top of St Clair Road. From Eagle Road it was open country – pasture land bordered by trees, with a few big houses set well back from the road. On the left, half-hidden by pines, there was the biggest house I'd seen in Warley. It was a mansion, in fact, a genuine Victorian mansion with turrets and battlements and a drive at least a quarter-of-a-mile long and a lodge at the gate as big as the average semi-detached.

'Who lives there?' I asked.

'Jack Wales,' George said. 'Or rather the Wales family. They bought it from a bankrupt woolman. Colossal, isn't it? Mind you they don't use half of it.'

My spirits sank. For the first time I realized Jack's colossal advantages. I thought that I was big and strong; but there was a lot more of that house than there was of me. It was a physical extension of Jack, at least fifty thousand pounds' worth of brick and mortar stating his superiority over me as a suitor.

The Aisgills' house stood at the end of a narrow dirt road just off St Clair Park. It was 1930 functional in white concrete, with a flat roof. There were no other houses near it and it stood on the top of a shelf of ground with the moors behind it and the park in front of it. It looked expensive, built-to-order, but out of place, like a Piccadilly tart walking the moors in high heels and nylons.

Inside it was decorated in white and off-white with steel and rubber chairs which were more comfortable than they appeared. There were three brightly coloured paintings on the walls: two of them were what seemed to me no more than a mix-up of lines and blobs and circles but the other was a recognizable portrait of Alice. She was wearing a low-cut evening dress in a glittering silver cloth. Her breasts were smaller and firmer and there were no lines on her face. The artist hadn't prettified her; I could see the faint heaviness of her chin and the beginnings of lines.

'Don't look at it too closely, Joe,' she said, coming up behind me. 'I was ten years younger then.'

'I wish I were ten years older,' I said.

'Why, Joe, that's very sweet of you.' She squeezed my hand, but didn't release it straightaway. 'You like the room?'

'Very much,' I said. But I wasn't quite sure that I did. It was a strange room, very clean, very bright, in good taste, but somehow without comfort. The low white-painted shelves across the wall opposite the fire-place were full of books, mostly brand-new, with their jackets still on; they should have humanized the room but they didn't; it seemed impossible that they should be read; they were so much a part of the room's decorative scheme that you wouldn't have dared to have taken one.

'Drink?' George asked, going to the cocktail cabinet. 'Gin, whisky, brandy, rum, sherry, and various loathsome liqueurs which I can't really recommend.'

'Whisky, please.'

He gave me a malicious look. 'It's not Scotch, alas. An American customer gave me a crate. Tastes like hair-oil. I warn you.'

'I drank a lot of it in Berlin,' I said. 'No soda, thanks.'

It left a warm glow inside my stomach after it had for a split second dried my mouth and sent a little rush of air up my throat.

'Alice says you're from Dufton.' He filled up his glass with soda-water and sipped it like a medicine.

'I was born there.'

'Been there on business once or twice. My God, it's depressing!'

'You get used to it.'

'You'll know the Torvers, I suppose.'

I did know them in the same way that I knew the Lord Lieutenant of the county. They were Dufton's oldest mill-owning family; in fact the only mill-owning family left after the Depression, the other mills having gone either into the hands of the Receiver or London syndicates.

'My father worked at their mill,' I said. 'He was an over-looker. So we never met socially, as you might say.'

George laughed. 'My dear Joe, no one ever meets the Torvers socially. No one would want to. The Old Man hasn't had one decent emotion since he was weaned, and Dicky Torver spends what little time he has left over from the mill-girls in drinking himself to death.'

'We used to call Dicky the Sexy Zombie,' I said.

'Damned good. I say, damned good!' He refilled my glass as if he were giving me a little reward for amusing him. 'That's *just* how he is with that awful pasty face and that slouch and that *fishy* gleam that comes into his eyes whenever he sees a bedworthy woman. Mind you, he's a good business man. You'd have to get up very early to catch Dicky Torver.'

'He's a horror,' said Alice, entering with a tray of sandwiches. She poured herself a whisky. 'I met him at the Con ball at Leddersford. He made a pass within the first five minutes and invited me to a dirty week-end within another five. Why doesn't someone beat him up?'

'Some women might find him attractive,' George said. He nibbled a cheese biscuit.

'You mean that their husbands might want to do business with him?' I said.

He laughed again. It was a low, pleasant laugh; he could evidently call it up at will. 'Not that way, Joe. It's like bribing an executioner; if you're reprieved, he says it's due to his efforts and if you're hanged you can't talk. If someone's wife is – well, *kind* to Dicky, and the husband lands the contract or whatever it is, then Dicky's kept his side of the bargain. If the husband doesn't land the contract he can hardly make a public complaint. No, business isn't as simple as all that.'

'It happens,' said Alice.

'Occasionally.' His manner indicated the subject was closed and I'd been put in my place.

'Joe,' Alice said, 'do have a sandwich. They're there to be eaten.'

The sandwiches were the thinnest possible slices of bread over thick slices of cold roast beef. The plate was piled high with them. 'You've cut up all your ration,' I said.

'Oh no,' she said. 'Don't worry about that. We've lots more. Truly.'

'The farmers have meat,' George said, 'I have cloth. See?'

It was perfectly clear, and I enjoyed the meat all the more. It was like driving Alice's car; for a moment I was living on the level I wanted to occupy permanently. I was the hero of one of those comedies with a title like *King for a Day*. Except that I couldn't have deceived myself as long as a day, and I could, in that room, tasting the undeniable reality of home-killed beef and feeling the whisky warm in my belly, put myself into George's shoes.

Alice was sitting a little away from the table, facing me. She was wearing a black pleated skirt and a bright red blouse of very fine poplin. She had very elegant legs, only an ounce away from scragginess; her likeness to a *Vogue* drawing struck me again. I looked at her steadily. We were the same sort of person, I thought fuzzily, fair and Nordic.

George poured me another Bourbon. I swallowed it and bit into a second sandwich. Alice gave me a light little smile. It was no more than a quick grimace, but I found my cheeks burning as I realized that I'd like to be in George's shoes in more ways than one.

DAVID STOREY
(1933–2017)

David Storey was a playwright, screenwriter, award-winning novelist and a professional rugby league player. He was born in Wakefield and had the ability to set down in elegiac prose the various eclectic elements of northern life in its many facets. He won the Booker Prize in 1976 for his novel *Saville*, which is the story of the life of Colin Saville, a miner's son, from his working-class Yorkshire childhood in the 1930s to his rise in the world, which leads him to be 'alienated from his class'. The novel creates a wonderful sense of time and place, as illustrated by the following passage, which describes a family holiday in Scarborough just before the outbreak of the Second World War. The bond between father and son is captured beautifully, as well as the evocation of the seaside town and its simple pleasures before the storm clouds gathered.

from Saville

The summer after the boy had started school they went away on holiday.

Colin had never seen the sea before; Saville had told him, during the weeks before they left, about its blueness, its size; about the sand, the gulls, the boats; about light-houses, even about smugglers. He'd heard about a lodging from a man at work; his wife had written; they'd sent a deposit. The day they left he got up early to find the boy already in the kitchen, cleaning his shoes, his clothes laid out on a chair by the empty grate, the two suitcases which they'd packed the night before already standing by the door.

'You're up early,' he said. 'Do you think they've got the train out yet? Yon engine, I think'll be having its breakfast.'

The boy had scarcely smiled; already there was that dull, almost sombre earnestness about him, melancholic, contained, as if it were some battle they were about to fight.

'Could you do mine up as well?' the father asked him.

Saville got his own shoes out, then got the breakfast, his wife still making the beds upstairs.

Later, when they set off, the boy had tried to lift the cases.

'Nay, you'll not shift those,' the father said. From the moment the boy had finished the shoes he'd been finding jobs, clearing the grate, emptying the ashes, helping to finish the washing-up, following his mother round as she inspected all the rooms, turning off the gas, checking the taps, making sure the window catches had been fastened tightly. They bolted and locked the back door then carried the cases to the front. Saville had set them in the garden, the patch of ground between the front door and the gate, and as he locked the door and tested it, and looked up at the windows, the boy had lifted first one case then the other then, finally, gasping, had put them down.

'Better let me carry those,' Saville said. He'd laughed. He gave his wife the key. 'Though I don't know why we're locking up. There's nought in there to pinch.'

Even then, with nothing to do but follow them, the boy's mood had scarcely changed; he held his mother's hand, looking over at his father, waiting impatiently, half-turned, while Saville rested, or switched the cases, trying one in one hand then the other.

'We've enough in here for a couple of months,' he told her. 'I mu'n have got a handcart if I'd known they were as heavy as this.'

It was still early. The streets were empty; the sky overhead was dark and grey. Earlier, looking out of the window, he'd said, 'Sithee, when it sees we're off on holiday, it'll start to brighten.' Yet, though they were now in the street and moving down, slowly, towards the station, it showed no sign of changing: if anything, the clouds had thickened.

'I should say no more about the weather,' his wife had said. 'The more you talk about the sun the less we'll see.'

'Don't worry. When it sees us on our way it'll start to brighten.' He glanced over at the boy. 'It likes to see people enjoying themselves,' he added.

At the end of each street Saville rested; at one point he lit a cigarette but soon abandoned it. Occasionally, as they passed the houses, they saw people stirring, curtains being drawn, fires lit; one or two people came to the doors.

'Off away, then, Harry?'

'Aye,' Saville said. 'I think for good.'

'Weight thy's carrying tha mu'n be a month in travelling.'

'A month I should think', Saville said, 'at least.'

A milkman came down the street with a horse and cart; he brought the jugs from each of the doorsteps to the back of the cart and ladled the milk out from the shiny, oval can. At the back of the cart hung a row of scoops, some with long handles, some like metal jugs.

He called and waved.

'I could do with that this morning,' Saville said.

He gestured at the cart.

'How far are you going?' the milkman said.

'Down to the station.'

'I'll give you a lift,' he said, 'if you like.'

His wife wasn't certain; she looked at the cans of milk; there was scarcely any room inside.

'Thy mu'n take the cases,' Saville said. 'We can easy walk.'

'I'll take you all, old lad,' the milkman said. 'I won't be a jiffy.'

He wore a black bowler hat and brown smock; they waited while he finished at the doors.

'Off to the coast, then, are you?' he asked them as he came back down the street.

'That's where we're off,' Saville said, looking at the boy.

'First time, is it?' the milkman said.

'That's right. First time.'

'I wish I wa' going with you.'

The milkman had red cheeks; his eyes, light blue, gazed out at them from under the brim of his hat.

'Jump in,' he said. 'I'll load your cases.'

His wife climbed up first, holding on to the flat, curved spar that served as a mudguard. She stood on one side, Saville on the other.

The boy, when the milkman lifted him in last, stood at the front, where the reins came into the cart over a metal bar.

The two cases, finally, were set in the middle, up-ended between the tall cans of milk.

'Now, then,' he said. 'We'll see if she can shift us.'

He took the reins, clicked his tongue, and the brown horse, darker even than the milkman's smock, started forward.

'Not too good weather yet,' the milkman said. He gestured overhead.

'It'll start to brighten,' Saville said. 'I've not known one day it's shone the day we left.'

'Start black: end bright. Best way to go about it,' the milkman said.

The horse clattered through the village. The cart, like a see-saw, swayed to and fro.

'They mu'n be wondering where I've got to.' The milkman gestured back. 'Usually on time, tha knows, within a couple of minutes.'

'It was good of you to bother,' Saville said.

'Nay, I wish I wa' coming with you. What's a hoss for if it can't be used?'

Colin clung to the metal bar in front; it was looped and curved: the reins came through a narrow eyelet. His head was scarcely higher than the horse's back.

Saville saw the way the boy's legs had tensed, the whiteness of his knuckles as he clutched the bar. He glanced over at his wife. She was standing sideways, pale-faced, her eyes wide, half-startled, clutching to the wooden rail with one hand and to the side of the cart with the other; she had on a hat the same colour as her coat, reddish brown, brimless, sweeping down below her ears.

The last of the houses gave way to fields; Saville could smell the freshness of the air. A lark was singing: he could see its dark speck against the cloud. Behind them the colliery chimney filtered out a stream of smoke, thin, blackish; there were sheep in one of the fields, and cattle.

In another, by itself, stood a horse. He pointed it out, calling to the boy.

Colin nodded. He stood by the milkman's much larger figure, looking round, not releasing the metal rail, his head twisted: Saville could see the redness of his cheeks, the same sombre, startled look that had overcome him as he was lifted in the cart.

'Thy mu'n say goodbye to them, tha knows,' he said. 'Tell 'em we're off on holiday.'

The milkman laughed.

'They'll have seen nothing as strange,' he added to his wife. 'Off on holiday on the back of a milkman's cart.'

The road dipped down to the station; the single track divided and went off in two deep cuttings across the fields.

The milkman turned the cart into the station yard; he got down first, helping Mrs Saville then the boy, then taking the cases as Saville held them out.

Saville got down himself. He dusted his coat.

'That's been very good of you,' his wife had said.

'Aye, it's helped us a lot. I don't know how long it'd have taken me to carry that lot.' Saville gestured back the way they'd come. 'We'd be still up yonder, I should think, for one thing; and for another, my arms might have easily dropped off after all that carrying.' He glanced over at the boy: he was gazing at the horse, then at the cart.

'Well, I wish you a good holiday, then,' the milkman said. He climbed into the cart and took the reins. 'Get back to me round afore they've noticed.'

'It's been very good of you,' his wife had said again.

They watched him turn the cart: he waved; the horse trotted out to the road then disappeared across the bridge.

'Well, that was a damn good turn. I suppose we shall have to wait though. It's put us thirty minutes early,' Saville said.

He took the cases over to the booking-hall. There was no one there. The bare wooden floor was dusty.

A planked walk took them through to a metal bridge: as they crossed over it they could see the rails below. A flight of stone steps, steep and narrow, took them down to the platform the other side.

He set the two cases down by a wooden seat.

'I'll go back up', he said, 'and get the tickets.'

Looking back from the booking-hall, he could see his wife and the boy standing by the cases; after one or two moments his wife sat down. The boy wandered over to the edge of the platform; he gazed down at the single track, looked up briefly towards the booking-hall, then turned and crossed the platform.

A goods train came slowly through the station; the bridge for a moment was hidden by smoke. The station itself had vanished; when the smoke had cleared his wife and the boy were standing at the edge of the platform watching the row of wagons pass.

The booking-clerk came through from an office at the rear: Saville paid for the tickets and, having re-crossed the bridge, went down the narrow steps and joined them.

The town had been built in the angle of a shallow bay. To the north, overlooking the houses, stood a ruined castle. It had been built on a peninsula of ochreish-looking rock which swung round, like a long arm, above the red-tiled roofs of the town itself; all that remained of the castle was a long, sprawling wall, and the dismembered section of a large, square-shaped keep. Around the foot of the headland formed by this peninsula ran a wide road, below which the sea boiled and frothed; even in calm weather it came up against the wall below the road in a heavy swell, following its sharply curved contour round to the shelter of the harbour on one side and to a broader, somewhat deeper bay to the north.

When the tide was out there were wide, sandy beaches. The house where they were staying lay to the south of the castle, near the harbour; from the upper windows they could see into the bay: they could see the white, glistening pleasure-boats as they churned in and out on their trips along the coast, and the fishing-smacks that lay in droves against the harbour wall, one fastened to another, and the crowds of people on the beach itself.

Saville had worked two weeks' overtime for his two weeks' holiday; instead of an eight-hour shift each day he'd worked sixteen hours, coming home exhausted to snatch a few hours' sleep. He still felt the tiredness now, an emptiness, as if his limbs and his mind had been hollowed out: it was a hulk that he took down to the beach each morning; it was a hulk that was slowly filled with the smell of the sea, with the smell of the fish on the harbour quay, of the sand. Even the sun, once they'd got there, had begun to shine. He felt a new life opening out before him, full of change; it was inconceivable to him now that he'd ever work beneath the ground again.

WINIFRED HOLTBY
(1898–1935)

South Riding is a novel by Winifred Holtby, published posthumously in 1936. The novel was edited by her close friend, Vera Brittain, author of *Testament of Youth*. The book is set in the fictional South Riding of Yorkshire, the inspiration being the East Riding where Holtby, a staunch feminist, was born and grew up. The central character is Sarah Burton, an idealistic young headmistress who, after working in London for a time, returns to Kiplington in Yorkshire to continue her career. To a large extent Sarah is based on Holtby's mother, Alice, who became the first alderwoman on the East Riding Council. In this extract, Sarah arrives back in Yorkshire.

from South Riding

MISS BURTON SURVEYS A BATTLEFIELD

A few days afterwards Miss Sarah Burton, emerging from the huge glass-covered arch of Kingsport Terminus, learned that the Kiplington bus was about to depart from the other side of the square.

With a leap, she was after it, her slim legs springing lightly, head up, chest out, small suitcase slapping her hip. She ran like a deer, dodging in and out of Kingsport citizens, nearly boarding the Dollstall bus by mistake, and finally sprinting the last fifty yards, clutching a rail, and swinging on to the Kiplington bus as it rounded Duke Street corner.

"Now, now, now!" cried the conductor. "Hold tight. What d'you think you're doing? Hundred yards championship?"

Sarah grinned amiably and sank on to the nearest seat, which she discovered to be the knee of a portly gentleman. She sprang up, apologetic. "*So* sorry."

"Not at all."

"He likes it," winked the avuncular conductor.

Sarah was about to wink back when she remembered that she was nearly forty and a head mistress.

She set down her case demurely and, climbing to the top of the bus, disposed of herself in a corner.

Well, well, well, she admonished. You've got to behave now. No more running after buses. No more little sleeveless cotton dresses. No more sitting on the knees of strange fat gentlemen. Dignity; solidity; stability. You've got to impress these people.

I'll have to buy a car. So long as I have to catch buses I shall run. I know it. I wonder if Derrick would sell me his for thirty pounds. He said he would once.

She pressed her bare strong hands together.

I must make a success of this, she told herself. I must justify it all. "All" meant the wrenching of herself away from South London, parting from Miss Tattersall, leaving her friends, her flat, her security—the delightful groove that she had hollowed for herself out of the great complicated mass of London—the Promenade Concerts, the political meetings, the breakfasts with Derrick, or Mick, or Tony, in summer dawns at the Ship, Greenwich. Once they had taken Tatters there for supper. On the top of the bus Sarah smiled again to remember Tatters watching the great ships gliding up London river, her round face flushed with excitement, a sausage speared on her fork, repeating firmly: "No more beer. Impossible, my boy, impossible. I'm a head mistress."

Tatters was a great woman and a darling.

But it had been time to get away. It was all too pleasant. It had been now or never. Another year or two and she could not have broken free. She would have stayed until Tatters retired, slipped into her place, and never never struck out for herself, nor built for herself till death.

She counted her slender assets: brains, will-power, organising ability, a hot temper, real enjoyment of teaching, a Yorkshire childhood. She counted her defects—her size, her flaming hair, her sense of humour, her tactlessness, her arrogance, her lack of dignity.

(All the same, Tatters had called her the best second mistress that she had ever known.) She must write and tell Tatters about her day's adventures. She began to frame in her mind a letter to her friend—one of those intimate descriptive letters which so rarely reach the paper. She would describe the Kingsport streets through which she rode, swaying and jolting.

Five minutes after leaving the station, her bus crossed a bridge and the walls opened for a second on to flashing water and masts and funnels where a canal from the Leame cut right into the city. Then the blank cliffs of warehouses, stores and offices closed in upon her. The docks would be beyond them. She must visit the docks. Ships, journeys, adventures were glorious to Sarah. The walls of this street were powdered from the fine white dust of flour mills and cement works. Tall cranes swung towering to Heaven. It's better than an inland industrial town, thought Sarah, and wished that the bus were roofless so that she might sniff the salty tarry fishy smell of docks instead of the petrol-soaked stuffiness of her glass and metal cage.

A bold-faced girl with a black fringe and blue ear-rings stood, arms on hips, at the mouth of an alley, a pink cotton overall taut across her great body, near her time, yet unafraid, gay, insolent.

Suddenly Sarah loved her, loved Kingsport, loved the

sailor or fish porter or whatever man had left upon her the proof of his virility.

After the London life she had dreaded return to the North lest she should grow slack and stagnant; but there could be no stagnation near these rough outlandish alleys.

The high walls of the warehouses diminished. She came to a street of little shops selling oilskins and dungarees and men's drill overalls, groceries piled with cheap tinned foods, grim crumbling façades announcing *Beds for Men* on placards foul and forbidding as gallow signs. On left and right of the thoroughfare ran mean monotonous streets of two-storied houses, bay-windowed and unvarying—not slums, but dreary respectable horrors, seething with life which was neither dreary nor respectable. Fat women lugged babies smothered in woollies; toddlers still sucking dummies tottered on bowed legs along littered pavements. Pretty little painted sluts minced on high tilted heels off to the pictures or dogs or dirt-track race-course.

I must go to the dogs again some time, Sarah promised herself. She had the gift of being pleased by any form of pleasure. It never surprised her when her Sixth Form girls deserted their homework for dancing, speed tracks or the films. She sympathised with them.

The road curved near to the estuary again. A group of huts and railway carriages were hung with strings of red and gold and green electric lights like garlands. The bus halted beside it. Sarah could read a notice "Amicable

Jack Brown's Open Air Café. Known in every Port in the World. Open all Night."

She was enchanted. Oh, I must come here. I'll bring the staff. It'll do us all good.

She saw herself drinking beer with a domestic science teacher among the sailors at two o'clock in the morning. The proper technique of headmistress-ship was to break all rules of decorum and justify the breach.

"Oh, lovely world," thought Sarah, in love with life and all its varied richness.

The bus stopped in a village for parcels and passengers, then emerged suddenly into the open country.

It was enormous.

So flat was the plain, so clear the August evening, so shallow the outspread canopy of sky, that Sarah, high on the upper deck of her bus, could see for miles the patterned country, the corn ripening to gold, the arsenic green of turnip tops, the tawny dun-colour of the sun-baked grass. From point to point on the horizon her eye could pick out the clustering trees and dark spire or tower marking a village. Away on her right gleamed intermittently the River Leame.

She drew a deep breath.

Now she knew where she was. This was her battlefield. Like a commander inspecting a territory before planning a campaign, she surveyed the bare level plain of the South Riding.

Sarah believed in action. She believed in fighting. She had unlimited confidence in the power of the human intelligence and will to achieve order, happiness, health and wisdom. It was her business to equip the young women entrusted to her by a still inadequately enlightened state for their part in that achievement. She wished to prepare their minds, to train their bodies, and to inoculate their spirits with some of her own courage, optimism and unstaled delight. She knew how to teach; she knew how to awaken interest. At the South London School she had initiated debates, clubs, visits, excursions to the Houses of Parliament, the London County Council, the National Portrait Gallery, the Tower of London, the Becontree Estate; she had organised amateur housing surveys and open-air performances of Euripides (in translation), she had supervised parents' conversaziones, "cabinet meetings," essay competitions, inquiries into public morals or imperial finance. Her official "subjects" were History and Civics, but all roads led to her Rome—an inexhaustible curiosity about the contemporary world and its inhabitants.

Her theories were, she felt, founded upon experience. She had known poverty; she had known hardship; she had watched her mother struggle triumphantly under the double burden of wage-earning and maternity; she had seen her sister, Pattie, crippled by a fall from her drunken father's arms in childhood, wring from life beauty and love and assurance and the marriage which she had always declared to be an essential condition of her happiness. She had herself abandoned a joyous expedition to Australia to make a home in England for her mother whose health had finally broken down. She had thought then her adventures over; she disapproved on principle of sacrifice; but she loved her mother, and had found at the South London School work which satisfied her and abundant friendships. Courage conquered circumstance. She thought that it could conquer everything.

Her turbulent strenuous vivid life had not been without vicissitudes. She had a habit, inconvenient in head mistresses, of falling in love misguidedly and often. She had been engaged to marry three different men. The first, a college friend, was killed on the Somme in 1916; the second, a South African farmer, irritated her with his political dogmatism until they quarrelled furiously and irreparably; the third, an English Socialist member of Parliament, withdrew in alarm when he found her feminism to be not merely academic but insistent. That affair had shaken her badly, for she loved him. When he demanded that she should abandon, in his political interests, her profession gained at such considerable public cost and private effort, she offered to be his mistress instead of his wife and found that he was even more shocked by this suggestion than by her previous one that she should continue her teaching after marriage. She parted from him with an anguish which amazed her, for she still thought of herself as a cold woman. Yet nothing that had happened to her had broken her self-confidence. She knew herself to be desirable and desired, withheld only from marriage by the bars of death or of principle. She had never loved without first receiving courtship; her person and her pride remained, she considered, under her own suzerainty.

She had even the successful woman's slight and half-conscious contempt for those less attractive than herself, only she felt that on her heart were tender places like bruises on an apple, which could not bear rough handling.

Well, I've done with all that, she thought, as the red and grey huddle of Kiplington spread itself into a fair-sized watering-place. No chance of a love-affair here in the South Riding and a good thing too. I was born to be a spinster, and by God, I'm going to spin.

I shall enjoy this. I shall build up a great school here. No one yet knows it except myself. I know it. I'll make the South Riding famous.

Four wretched houses. A sticky board of governors. A moribund local authority. A dead end of nowhere. That's my material. I shall do it.

The bus turned a corner into the square containing the Municipal Gardens and Bowling Green—an oblong of weary turf surrounded by asphalt paths and iron railings.

"All change!" shouted the conductor.

Sarah climbed down and retrieved her suitcase.

"Can you tell me my way to the Cliff Hotel?" she asked.

"It's a good walk."

"I'm a good walker."

"You'll find that case heavy."

"That's my business."

"If I were a single man and out of a job, I'd carry it for you."

"I'll take the will for the deed," Sarah twinkled, still, in spite of her heroic resolutions, pleased by opportunities for flirtatious back-chat.

She extracted directions from the man and set off walking briskly through her new domain.

Kiplington was taking its evening pleasures.

Along the esplanade strolled couples chewing spearmint, smoking gaspers, sucking oranges. All forms of absorption, mastication and inhalation augmented the beneficent effect of sea air, slanting sun and holiday leisure. Mothers with laden paper carriers and aching varicose veins pushed prams back to hot crowded lodgings; elderly gentlemen in nautical blue jackets leaned on iron railings and turned telescopes intended for less personal objects upon the charms of Kingsport nymphs emerging from their final bathe. The tide was coming in, a lid of opaque grey glass sliding quietly over littered shingle. Sarah felt suddenly aware of the heat and grime of her long journey.

She ran down the steps and hired a bathing tent.

Five minutes later she was wading out into the agreeable salty chill of the North Sea.

It did not worry her that her fellow bathers were spotted youths from Kingsport back streets and little girls with rat-tailed hair from the Catholic Holiday Home. It did not worry her that the narrowing sands were dense with sweating, jostling, sucking, shouting humanity, that the sea-wall was scrawled with ugly chalk-marks, that the town beyond the wall was frankly hideous. This was her own place. These were her own people.

She swam with blissful leisurely strokes out to sea, then turned and floated, looking back with satisfaction at the flat ugly face of the town, the apartment houses, the dust-blown unfinished car-park, the pretentious desolation of the barn-like Floral Hall.

Away to her right she could see the red crumbling road of the higher North Cliff, and the group of houses among which was her new school—"Until I get something better," she promised herself, lying back and kicking the water happily.

Then she remembered that she wore no bathing cap, cursed the tangled profusion of her springing hair which took so long to dry, and swam reluctantly, slowly, back to shore.

A breakwater of soft satiny wood polished by a thousand tides ran down to the sea. Taking the hired towel, Sarah perched herself on one of its weed-grown stumps and sat in her brief green bathing dress, one foot in the water, drying her hair and whistling, not quite unaware that Mr. Councillor Alfred Ezekiel Huggins, haulage contractor, Wesleyan Methodist lay preacher, found in her pretty figure a matter for contemplation. He propped his plump stomach against the sun-warmed paling, and remained there, enjoying the pose of her slim muscular body, her lifted arms, her hair like a flaming cresset. From that distance he could not see her physical defects, her hands and head too big, her nose too aggressive, her eyes too light, her mouth too obstinate. Nor did he dream that here was the head mistress whose appointment he, as a member of the Higher Education Sub-Committee, had recently sanctioned.

Sarah, her hair dry enough, the tide within ten yards of her tent, slid off the breakwater and went in to dress. Aware of approving eyes upon her, she increased, unconsciously and almost imperceptibly, the slight swagger of her walk. She was her father's daughter.

J. B. PRIESTLEY
(1894–1984)

J. B. Priestley was born in Bradford, a city which stayed in his blood and often found voice in his writings. He enjoyed great success with his novels and later with plays such as *An Inspector Calls* and *Time and the Conways*. It was in the opening pages of his novel *The Good Companions* (1929) that he was able to distil the essence of Yorkshire as he knew it in the 1920s. He presents vivid images of the fictitious town of Bruddersford (a blending of Bradford and Huddersfield) that are not only rich in detail, atmosphere and wonderful sense of place but had a relevance and verisimilitude that remained until the 1950s, when the town planners rolled out their modernizing schemes, which involved demolishing and sweeping away much that gave rich individual character to these Yorkshire towns and cities. Jess Oakroyd, one of the leading characters in the novel, would not recognize Bruddersford today, but thankfully Priestley has retained its fascinating beauty in literary aspic.

from The Good Companions

MR OAKROYD LEAVES HOME

There, far below, is the knobbly backbone of England, the Pennine Range. At first, the whole dark length of it, from the Peak to Cross Fell, is visible. Then the Derbyshire hills and the Cumberland fells disappear, for you are descending, somewhere about the middle of the range, where the high moorland thrusts itself between the woollen mills of Yorkshire and the cotton mills of Lancashire. Great winds blow over miles and miles of ling and bog and black rock, and the curlews still go crying in that empty air as they did before the Romans came. There is a glitter of water here and there, from the moorland tarns that are now called reservoirs. In summer you could wander here all day, listening to the larks, and never meet a soul. In winter you could lose your way in an hour or two and die of exposure perhaps, not a dozen miles from where the Bradford trams end or the Burnley trams begin. Here are Bodkin Top and High Greave and Black Moor and Four Gates End, and though these are lonely places, almost unchanged since the Domesday Book was compiled, you cannot understand industrial Yorkshire and Lancashire, the wool trade and the cotton trade and many other things besides, such as the popularity of Handel's *Messiah* or the Northern Union Rugby game, without having seen such places. They hide many secrets. Where the moor thins out are patches of ground called 'Intake', which means that they are land wrested from the grasp of the moor. Over to the right is a long smudge of smoke, beneath which the towns of the West Riding lie buried, and fleeces, tops, noils, yarns, stuffs, come and go, in and out of the mills, down to the railways and canals and lorries. All this too, you may say, is a kind of Intake.

At first the towns only seem a blacker edge to the high moorland, so many fantastic outcroppings of its rock, but now that you are closer you see the host of tall chimneys, the rows and rows of little houses, built of blackening stone, that are like tiny sharp ridges on the hills. These windy moors, these clanging dark valleys, these factories and little stone houses, this business of Intaking, have between them bred a race that has special characteristics. Down there are thousands and thousands of men and women who are stocky and hold themselves very stiffly, who have short upper lips and long chins, who use emphatic consonants and very broad vowels and always sound aggressive, who are afraid of nothing but mysterious codes of etiquette and any display of feeling. If it were night, you would notice strange con-stellations low down in the sky and little golden beetles climbing up to them. These would be street lamps and lighted tramcars on the hills, for here such things are little outposts in No Man's Land and altogether more adventurous and romantic than ordinary street lamps and tramcars. It is not night, however, but a late Sep-tember afternoon. Some of its sunshine lights up the nearest of the towns, most of it jammed into a narrow

valley running up to the moors. It must be Bruddersford, for there, where so many roads meet, is the Town
Hall, and if you know the district at all you must immediately recognize the Bruddersford Town Hall, which
has a clock that plays *Tom Bowling* and *The Lass of
Richmond Hill*. It has been called 'a noble building in
the Italian Renaissance style' and always looks as if it
had no right to be there.

Yes, it is Bruddersford. Over there is the enormous
factory of Messrs Holdsworth and Co. Ltd, which has
never been called a noble building in any style but
nevertheless looks as if it had a perfect right to be
there. The roof of the Midland Railway Station glitters
in the sun, and not very far away is another glitter from
the glass roof of the Bruddersford Market Hall, where,
securely under cover, you may have a ham tea or buy
boots and pans and mint humbugs and dress lengths
and comic songs. That squat bulk to the left of the Town
Hall is the Lane End Congregational Chapel, a monster
that can swallow any two thousand people who happen
to be in search of 'hearty singing and a bright service'.
That streak of slime must be the Leeds and Liverpool
Canal or the Aire and Calder Canal, one of the two.
There is a little forest of mill chimneys. Most of them
are only puffing meditatively, for it is Saturday afternoon and nearly four hours since the workpeople
swarmed out through the big gates. Some of the chimneys show no signs of smoke; they have been quiet for
a long time, have stayed there like monuments of an age
that has vanished, and all because trade is still bad.

Perhaps some of these chimneys have stopped smoking because fashionable women in Paris and London and New York have cried to one another, 'My dear, you can't possibly wear that!' and less fashionable women have repeated it after them, and quite unfashionable women have finally followed their example, and it has all ended in machines lying idle in Bruddersford. Certainly, trade is still very bad. But as you look down on Bruddersford, you feel that it will do something about it, that it is only biding its time, that it will hump its way through somehow: the place wears a grim and resolute look. Yet this afternoon it is not thinking about the wool trade.

Something very queer is happening in that narrow thoroughfare to the west of the town. It is called Manchester Road because it actually leads you to that city, though in order to get there you will have to climb to the windy roof of England and spend an hour or two with the curlews. What is so queer about it now is that the road itself cannot be seen at all. A grey-green tide flows sluggishly down its length. It is a tide of cloth caps.

These caps have just left the ground of the Bruddersford United Association Football Club. Thirty-five thousand men and boys have just seen what most of them call 't'United' play Bolton Wanderers. Many of them should never have been there at all. It would not be difficult to prove by statistics and those mournful little budgets (How a Man May Live – or rather, avoid death – on Thirty-five Shillings a Week) that seem to attract some minds, that these fellows could not afford the entrance fee. When some mills are only working half the week and others not at all, a shilling is a respectable sum of money. It would puzzle an economist to discover where all these shillings came from. But if he lived in Bruddersford, though he might still wonder where they came from, he would certainly understand why they were produced. To say that these men paid their shillings to watch twenty-two hirelings kick a ball is merely to say that a violin is wood and catgut, that *Hamlet* is so much paper and ink. For a shilling the Bruddersford United A.F.C. offered you Conflict and Art; it turned you into a critic, happy in your judgement of fine points, ready in a second to estimate the worth of a well-judged pass, a run down the touch line, a lightning shot, a clearance kick by back or goalkeeper; it turned you into a partisan, holding your breath when the ball came sailing into your own goalmouth, ecstatic when your forwards raced away towards the opposite goal, elated, downcast, bitter, triumphant by turns at the fortunes of your side, watching a ball shape Iliads and Odysseys for you; and, what is more, it turned you into a member of a new community, all brothers together for an hour and a half, for not only had you escaped from the clanking machinery of this lesser life, from work, wages, rent, doles, sick pay, insurance cards, nagging wives, ailing children, bad bosses, idle workmen, but you had escaped with most of your mates and your neighbours, with half the town, and there you were, cheering together, thumping one another on the shoulders, swopping judgements like lords of the earth, having pushed your way through a turnstile into another and altogether more splendid kind of life, hurtling with Conflict and yet passionate and beautiful in its Art. Moreover, it offered you more than a shilling's worth of material for talk during the rest of the week. A man who had missed the last home match of 't'United' had to enter social life on tiptoe in Bruddersford.

Somewhere in the middle of this tide of cloth caps is one that is different from its neighbours. It is neither grey nor green but a rather dirty brown. Then, unlike most of the others, it is not too large for its wearer, but, if anything, a shade too small, though it is true he has pushed it back from his forehead as if he were too hot – as indeed he is. This cap and the head it has almost ceased to decorate are both the property of a citizen of Bruddersford, an old and enthusiastic supporter of the United Football Club, whose name is Jesiah Oakroyd. He owes his curious Christian name to his father, a lanky weaving over-looker who divided his leisure, in alternating periods of sin and repentance, between The Craven Arms and the Lane End Primitive Methodist Chapel, where he chanced to hear the verse from First *Chronicles*, 'Of the sons of Uzziel; Micah the first, and Jesiah the second,' the very day before his second son was born. To all his intimates, however, Mr Oakroyd is known as 'Jess'. He is a working man between forty-five and fifty years of age, a trifle under medium height but stockily built, neither ugly nor handsome, with a blunt nose, a moustache that may have been once brisk and fair but is now ragged and mousey, and blue eyes that regard the world pleasantly enough but with just a trace of either wonder or resentment or of both. He lives almost in the shadow of two great factories, in one of those districts known locally as 'back o' t'mill', to be precise, at 51 Ogden Street. He has lived there these last twenty years, and is known to the whole street as a quiet man and a decent neighbour. He is on his way there now, returning from the match to his Saturday tea, which takes a high rank in the hierarchy of meals, being perhaps second only to Sunday dinner. He has walked this way, home from the match, hundreds of times, but this Saturday in late September is no ordinary day for him – although he does not know it – for it is the very threshold of great events. Chance and Change are preparing an ambush. Only a little way before him there dangles invitingly the end of a thread. He must be followed and watched.

H. P. KENDALL
(1875–1937)

There is no place on the Yorkshire coast that has been visited by such a range of significant writers over the years as Whitby, particularly in the nineteenth century. These scribes found something special in Whitby and its environment; it was a place to relax, enjoy a holiday and for some it was an inspiration for their writing. H. P. Kendall, a local author himself, made a record of these visits in his little pamphlet *Whitby in Literature*, originally published around 1913.

from Whitby in Literature

Amongst the most notable associations with Whitby is that of the Du Maurier family. George Du Maurier was one of the best known of the celebrated artists of "Punch" during a long association with that journal, and he was also author of three novels, one of which, "Trilby," was afterwards dramatised with phenomenal success. The name survives to-day in the "Trilby Hat." For many years he was a well-known figure in Whitby during the annual holidays of his family, his inseparable companion being a large St. Bernard dog named "Chang." The Du Mauriers stayed at No. 1 St. Hilda's Terrace, and also at No. 9 Broomfield Terrace.

In "Gerald," by Daphne Du Maurier, we are brought into intimate touch with the family circle; how they planned the delights of that annual holiday in Whitby, "an ever-increasing joy, when the days were never long enough; watching Papa draw, and skilfully inveigling from Mummie the promise of a new tennis racket."

When George Du Maurier was thoroughly enjoying himself on the sands, his wife would dash at him with a wretched muffler, and wind it round his throat, or make them all take jerseys and overcoats when they left the rooms in St. Hilda's Terrace for the tennis courts.

"What fun Whitby was, though! What an unending delight and discovery, with the big seas that broke over the end of the pier, and the slime and smell of herrings and cod in the fish market; and bathing and cricket on the sands, tennis tournaments, picnics on the moors, with Mummie clinging to her hat and her skirt, and Trixie, too, while Papa smoked and sketched, and Guy read, and Gerald and Sylvia and May scampered about in the heather with 'Chang' padding slowly at their heels."

[...]

In the year 1903, Gerald Du Maurier spent his honeymoon at Whitby, in the month of April. He had not visited here since the death of his father (October, 1896), and he wished his wife to see the place where he had spent so many happy hours.

"He wanted her to know the old rooms where they used to go every year, and the harbour where Papa had strolled with 'Chang' padding at his heels, and the broad-hipped fisherwomen had paused to smile at him; the red roofs, and the cobbled stones, the salty, fishy, spray-laden Whitby air, with its tang of cutch and rope yarn, nets and herrings. Here was the place where he had learnt to swim . . . and there was the road that led to the moors . . . But here was his Whitby, unchanged and best beloved as of old; and the little span of years rolled back, and he was a boy again."

In 1917 he was back again. The war had frayed his nerves, and he was obviously unhappy. His favourite brother had been killed, and the strain of an emotional part in the play, "Dear Brutus," had been too great a tax on him.

"It was surely a mistake to go to Whitby for a

holiday; he might have realised that every corner held a ghost, and every twist and turning of the narrow cobbled streets was haunted by memories. There was an echo in the cry of the gulls, and other footsteps followed his upon the quay.

The skies were grey, and the sea wind-blown and cold; the waves broke upon the beach and against the pier with a shudder and a cry of lament."

He was staying at a hotel on this occasion, and was a haunted man struggling with the phantoms of the past.

"He must never come here again, never, never. There were too many voices, and sometimes they called so loud he had to stand quite still."

Even the presence of his wife and children could not banish the feeling of loneliness, for memories stifled him. On this note of weariness ended the connection of the Du Mauriers, father and son, with Whitby.

In the sketches he drew for "Punch," George Du Maurier often introduced the figures of his wife and daughters with a Whitby background easily recognisable. As an instance, the old cast-iron seats, of which a few survive along the West Pier, appear in some of the drawings, whilst other little details occur, some of which can be seen amongst the artist's original work in the Pannett Art Gallery.

The following appeared in a letter to the Press in 1934, just a hundred years after George Du Maurier was born:

"In that wonderful Jubilee year (August 28th, 1887,

to be exact) Du Maurier led across the cliffs to the adjacent Robin Hood's Bay (an even quainter little fishing port) two famous Americans—James Russell Lowell and Henry James. Lowell was for some years until 1885 the United States Ambassador to London, and the latter was still resident in Boston, and had not yet become a British citizen and an O.M.

"All three signed the visitors' book in the inn on the cliff edge, Du Maurier with a touch of his pen depicting a couple of figures gleefully disporting themselves in the open."

Of George Du Maurier, Joseph Hatton, the writer, novelist and clever journalist, writes:

"It was never my privilege to see much of Du Maurier. I met him for the first time at Whitby, whereabouts, by the way, I gained my first experience of Yorkshire moors. Du Maurier was full of life and spirit, as his pictures of the Whitby fisherfolk in 'Punch' amply demonstrate. Mr. Smalley, the famous Anglo-American newspaper correspondent and essayist, was there, with princely Henry Irving. Being appealed to by the local circus manager, who was in bad circumstances, Irving bought up all the front seats, gave his friends a dinner at the hotel, and took them to the circus. On another night, it was a company of strolling players who needed Irving's patronage, and got it. What good is money except for the happiness it enables you to give to others? Monte Cristo could not be more lavish than Irving where his heart and his sympathy for his fellow-artistes were concerned.

Mrs. Du Maurier was a very English picture on the Quay at Whitby, where she went to the daily auction to buy her fish, and thus became the central figure of more than one of her husband's charming sketches in 'Punch.' It was a great sight to see the fishermen come in with their heavily-laden smacks. Fine fellows, these harvesters of the seas!"

Joseph Hatton was in Whitby in 1886, with that great friend of Sir Henry Irving's, John Lawrence Toole, the most popular comedian of his time. Hatton had previously stayed here with Irving, and of the latter he writes:

"It was autumn . . . somewhat stormy, too, and cold . . . we strolled into the night when Whitby was abed, and listened to the warning bell that boomed in the moaning waters off the coast; a gloomy yet fascinating sound at night, with the sea in darkness—only a strange void and blackness to tell us that it was writhing and tossing at our feet, and the bell moaning of rocks or shoals or other hidden dangers upon which, in the olden days, many a stalwart mariner had come to grief, with its funeral music in his ears."

These are the words of Hatton, and were perhaps inspired by his companionship that night—words that might well have come from the great tragedian himself. In any case, it is a striking word picture, as applicable to-day as it was then.

On Sir Henry Irving's last visit to Whitby he stayed at the Hotel Metropole.

In "An Artist's Reminiscences," by Walter Crane (1907), we find that celebrated artist visiting Whitby in the summer of 1875, and meeting his old friend, J. R. Wise.

"My wife and I had taken our little ones to Whitby for a few weeks, and were much charmed by the red-roofed fishing town below the green slopes, with the ruined Abbey and church on the hill above.

One day, walking towards Sandsend, I saw the well-known and rather unusual-looking figure on the road some way in front . . . I found he had been living in retirement at a remote farmhouse near Sandsend, carrying on his literary work. He did a good deal of reviewing for the 'Westminster Review,' the 'Saturday,' and other journals."

In the "Memorials of Edward Burne-Jones," by G. B-J., occurs the following:

"The children and I were then staying at Whitby" . . . He writes to the child . . . "I very much liked the little red picture you made for me of Whitby—it was better than I made at your age, and I want you to look at every lovely thing in the world and remember it, and forget about the rest."

These are the words of the man who painted beautiful women, and modelled his work on that of Rosetti, an influence responsible for bright colouring and a certain mysticism. His work stands alone for design and charm.

"The reason for our being at far-off Whitby was a suggestion of George Eliot's, that the children and I should take our seaside holiday there to meet her and

Mrs. Lewes. Our rooms were near them, and we met daily—a pleasure that atoned for the long journey."

Sir Edward Burne-Jones designed the figures for the celebrated tapestries of William Morris, and Whitby is fortunate in possessing two examples of these valuable works, they having being purchased by the late County Alderman R. E. Pannett, and bequeathed to the town.

From the above extracts we gather that Mrs. Burne-Jones was in company with George Eliot, the author of "Adam Bede," "Silas Marner," the "Mill on the Floss," and other novels which are now classics. Under the pen name of George Eliot, Miss Evans, afterwards Mrs. Cross, delighted thousands of Victorian readers. She died in 1880, so the visit was previous to that year. Georgina Burne-Jones, the writer of the Memoirs just quoted, was an aunt of the late Rudyard Kipling, and it may be of interest to mention that the house standing at the head of Haggersgate, now used by the "Missions to Seamen," was, in 1817, occupied by a Mr. Richard Rudyard, a member of the family from which the famous poet and writer of national ditties derived his Christian name.

[...]

Wilkie Collins was another writer who found the quiet of Whitby and district to his taste. In "No Name" (1862) he writes:

"We are residing in the secluded village of Ruswarp, on the banks of the Esk, about two miles inland from Whitby. Our lodgings are comfortable, and we possess the additional blessing of a tidy landlady."

His masterpieces of fiction, "The Woman in White,"

and "The Moonstone," are perhaps the ones by which he is best known; but he wrote some of his best stories for "Household Words" and "All the Year Round." He was for many years associated with Charles Dickens. A letter from Charles Dickens to Wilkie Collins, whilst the latter was staying in Whitby, in 1861, says:

"Likewise Sir, I have posted to Whitby. Pity the sorrows of a poor old man."

[...]

It is not generally known, I think, that C. L. Dodgson, known to all children, young or old, was one of Whitby's visitors, staying at No. 5 East Terrace, at the house of Mrs. Hunton. On one of these visits he wrote part of that famous classic, "Alice in Wonderland," whilst seated on the sands with a writing pad on his knee. Well might he be inspired to write:

"The Walrus and the Carpenter
Were walking close at hand,
They wept like anything to see
Such multitudes of sand."

"Alice in Wonderland" was published in 1865, but Whitby has the honour of earlier associations, for the author stayed at the above address from July to September of the year 1854. He was then twenty-two years of age, and probably studying for his degree of B.A. His first essays in literature, so far as is known, were made in the "Whitby Gazette," at that time a small paper devoted mainly to a list of visitors, but issuing gratis a small literary supplement. One of these supplements, dated August 31st, 1854, contains a humorous poem,

"The Lady of the Ladle," the concluding portion of which is a "Coronach," or lament, which runs as follows in the opening lines:

"She is gone by the Hilda,
She is lost unto Whitby,
And her name is Matilda,
Which my heart it was smit by;
Tho' I take the Goliah,
I learn to my sorrow
"That 'It won't,' says the crier,
'Be off till to-morrow'."

The "Hilda" and the "Goliah," were the two steamboats of the Whitby and Robin Hood's Bay Steam Packet Company.

This was followed by "Wilhelm von Schmitz," published in the "Whitby Gazette" supplement from September 7th to the 28th inclusive, one chapter appearing in each of the four supplements. It is a travesty of the popular short story of the period, concerning the love of a poet for a barmaid in Whitby, the third person being a very much hyphenated waiter. The opening sentences will convey some idea of the style in which the story is written:

"The sultry glare of noon was already giving place to the cool of a cloudless evening, and the lulled ocean was washing against the distant pier with a low murmur, suggestive to poetical minds of the kindred ideas of motion and lotion, when two travellers might have been seen, by such as chose to look that way, approaching the secluded town of Whitby by one of those headlong paths, dignified by the name of road, which serve as entrances into the place, and which were originally constructed, it is supposed, on the somewhat fantastic model of pipes running into a water-butt."

The poet's effusion to his inamorata shows that whimsical versification he eventually made his own:

"What though the world be cross and crooky?

Of Life's fair flowers the fairest bouquet

I plucked, when I chose thee, my Sukie."

The above effusions are signed simply "B.B.", for he had not then assumed the nom-de-plume by which he became famous as "Lewis Carroll." Apart from his books for children, he published several valuable treatises on mathematics, but "Alice's Adventures in Wonderland," and "Through the Looking-Glass," are what his fame now rests upon.

ALAN BENNETT
(*b.* 1934)

Leeds-born Alan Bennett is a national treasure. He first came to fame with the *Beyond the Fringe* revue in 1960, along with Peter Cook, Dudley Moore and Jonathan Miller. By the mid-sixties he had produced his first stage play, *Forty Years On*, which was a satirical excursion into public school life and what Bennett perceived as the erosion of standards in British society since the war. From then on, he never looked back. More plays and films followed, including *The Madness of King George III*, *The History Boys* and *The Lady in the Van* and the remarkable television series of one person plays, *Talking Heads*. However, in all this time Bennett never lost his Yorkshire accent nor his northern connections; he moved to London but he still kept a retreat in the Yorkshire Dales where he could escape the hurly-burly of city life. In 1994, he published *Writing Home*, a collection of essays from which the following piece is taken. It harks back to his youth in the Second World War and is charming for its humour and period detail.

from Writing Home

LEEDS TRAMS

There was a point during the Second World War when my father took up the double bass. To recall the trams of my boyhood is to be reminded particularly of that time.

It is around 1942 and we are living in the house my parents bought when they got married, 12 Halliday Place in Upper Armley. The Hallidays are handily situated for two tram routes, and if we are going into town, rather than to Grandma's in Wortley, the quickest way is to take a number 14. This means a walk across Ridge Road, down past the back of Christ Church (and Miss Marsden's the confectioner's) to Stanningley Road. Stanningley Road is already a dual carriageway because the tram tracks running down the middle of the road are pebbled and enclosed by railings, so splitting what little traffic there is into lanes. The Stanningley trams are generally somewhat superior to those on other routes, more upholstered, and when the more modern streamlined variety comes in after the war, it is more likely to be found on this route than elsewhere. But the drawback with the Stanningley Road trams is that they come down from Bramley or even Rodley, and are always pretty crowded, so more often than not we go for the other route, the number 16, which means walking up Moorfield Road to Charleycake Park and Whingate Junction.

This being the terminus, the tram is empty and as likely as not waiting, or, if we've just missed one, the next will already be in sight, swaying up Whingate. We wait as the driver swings outside and with a great twang hauls over the bogey ready for the journey back, while upstairs the conductor strolls down the aisle, reversing the seats before winding back the indicator on the front. The driver and conductor then get off and have their break sat on the form by the tram-stop, the driver generally older and more solid than the conductor (or, I suppose, the conductress, though I don't recall conductresses coming in until after the war).

Dad is a smoker, so we troop upstairs rather than going 'inside', the word a reminder of the time when upstairs was also outside. On some trams in 1942 it still is, because in these early years of the war a few open-ended trams have been brought back into service. We wedge ourselves in the front corner to be exposed to the wind and weather, an unexpected treat, and also an antidote to the travel sickness from which both my brother and I suffer, though I realize now that this must have been due as much to all the smoking that went on as to the motion of the tram itself. Neither of us ever actually is sick, but it's not uncommon and somewhere on the tram is a bin of sand just in case.

So the four of us – Mam, Dad, my brother and me – are ensconced on the tram sailing down Tong Road into town or, if we are going to see Grandma, who lives in the Gilpins, we will get off halfway at Fourteenth Avenue.

Around 1942, though, we come into the double-bass

period, when some of our tram journeys become fraught with embarrassment. Dad is a good amateur violinist, largely self-taught, so taking up the double bass isn't such a big step. He practises in the front room, which is never used for anything else, and, I suppose because the bass never has the tune, it sounds terrible; he sounds as if he's sawing (which he also does, actually, as one of his other hobbies is fretwork). Though the speaking 'that thing' isn't allowed on the tram at all. So while we sit inside and pretend he isn't with us, Dad stands on the platform grasping the bass by the neck as if he's about to give a solo. He gets in the way of the conductor, he gets in the way of the people getting on and off, and, always a mild man, it must have been more embarrassing for him than it ever was for us.

Happily this dance-band phase, like the fretwork and the herb beer, doesn't last long. He gets bored with the fretwork, the herb beer regularly explodes in the larder, and the double bass is eventually advertised in the Miscellaneous column of the *Evening Post* and we can go back to sitting on the top deck again.

After the war we move to Far Headingley, where Dad, having worked all his life for the Co-op, now has a shop of his own just below the tram-sheds opposite St Chad's. We live over the shop, so I sleep and wake to the sound of trams: trams getting up speed for the hill before Weetwood Lane, trams spinning down from West Park, trams shunted around in the sheds in the middle of the night, the scraping of wheels, the clanging of the bell.

It is not just the passage of time that makes me invest

the trams of those days with such pleasure. To be on a tram sailing down Headingley Lane on a fine evening lifted the heart at the time just as it does in memory. I went to school by tram, the fare a halfpenny from St Chad's to the Ring Road. A group of us at the Modern School scorned school dinners and came home for lunch, catching the tram from another terminus at West Park. We were all keen on music and went every Saturday to hear the Yorkshire Symphony Orchestra in the Town Hall, and it was on a tram at West Park that another sixth-former, 'Fanny' Fielder, sang to me the opening bars of Brahms's Second Piano Concerto, which I'd never heard and which the YSO was playing that coming Saturday. Trams came into that too, because after the concert many of the musicians went home by instrument is large the repertoire is small, except in one area: swing. Until now Dad has never had much time for swing, or popular music generally; his idea of a good time is to turn on the Home Service and play along with the hymns on *Sunday Half Hour*, or (more tentatively) with the light classics that are the staple of Albert Sandler and his Palm Court Orchestra. But now, with Dad in the grip of this new craze, Mam, my brother and I are made to gather round the wireless, tuned these days to the Light Programme, so that we can listen to dance-band music.

'Listen, Mam. Do you hear the beat? That's the bass. That'll be me.'

Dad has joined a part-time dance band. Even at eight years old I know that this is not a very good idea and just another of his crazes (the fretwork, the home-made beer) – schemes Dad has thought up to make a bit of money. So now we are walking up Moorfield Road to get the tram again, only this time to go and watch Dad play in his band somewhere in Wortley, and our carefree family of four has been joined by a fifth, a huge and threatening cuckoo, the double bass.

Knowing what is to happen, the family make no attempt to go upstairs, but scuttle inside while Dad begins to negotiate with the conductor. The conductor spends a lot of his time in the little cubby-hole under the winding metal stairs. There's often a radiator here that he perches on, and it's also where the bell-pull hangs, in those days untouchable by passengers, though it's often no fancier than a knotted leather thong. In his cubby-hole the conductor keeps a tin box with his spare tickets and other impedimenta which at the end of the journey he will carry down to the other end of the tram. The niche that protects the conductor from the pas-sengers is also just about big enough to protect the double bass, but when Dad suggests this there is invari-ably an argument, which he never wins, the clincher generally coming when the conductor points out that strictly tram (though none with a double bass), sitting there, rather shabby and ordinary and often with tab ends in their mouths, worlds away from the Delius, Walton and Brahms which they had been playing. It was a first lesson to me that art doesn't have much to do with appearances, and that ordinary middle-aged men in raincoats can be instruments of the sublime.

Odd details about trams come back to me now, like the slatted platforms, brown with dust, that were slung underneath either end, like some urban cowcatcher; or the little niche in the glass of the window on the seat facing the top of the stairs so that you could slide it open and hang out; and how convivial trams were, the seats reversible so that if you chose you could make up a four whenever you wanted.

How they work was always a mystery. As a child I had difficulty in understanding that the turning motion the driver made with the handle was what drove the tram, it seeming more like mixing than driving. And then there was the imposing demeanour of the ticket inspectors, invested with a spurious grandeur on a par with the one-armed man who showed you to your seat in Schofield's Café, or the manager of the Cottage Road cinema in his dinner-jacket, or gents' outfitters in general.

I don't recall anyone ever collecting tram numbers, but the route numbers had a certain mystique, the even numbers slightly superior to the odd, which tended to belong to trams going to Gipton, Harehills, or Belle Isle, parts of Leeds where I'd never ventured. And Kirkstall will always be 4, just as Lawnswood is 1.

Buses have never inspired the same affection – too comfortable and cushioned to have a moral dimension. Trams were bare and bony, transport reduced to its basic elements, and they had a song to sing, which buses never did. I was away at university when they started to phase them out, Leeds as always in too much of a hurry to get to the future, and so doing the wrong thing. I knew at the time that it was a mistake, just as Beeching was a mistake, and that life was starting to get nastier. If trams ever come back, though, they should come back not as curiosities, nor, God help us, as part of the heritage, but as a cheap and sensible way of getting from point A to point B, and with a bit of poetry thrown in.

Permissions Acknowledgements

Extract from *All Creatures Great and Small* by James Herriot © The James Herriot Partnership, published by Pan Macmillan, reproduced by permission of David Higham Associates.

'Pike' by Ted Hughes from *Selected Poems 1957–1967* published by Faber and Faber Ltd.

'Enjoy the Game' and 'No Bread' © Ian McMillan.

Extract from *A Kestrel for a Knave* by Barry Hines. Copyright © 1968, Barry Hines. Reprinted by permission of Penguin Books Limited.

Extract from *Room at the Top* by John Braine, published by Penguin Books, reproduced by permission of David Higham Associates.

Extract from *Billy Liar* by Keith Waterhouse, published by Penguin Books, reproduced by permission of David Higham Associates.

'Cædmon's Hymn' from *The Earliest English Poems* by Michael Alexander, published by Penguin Classics. Copyright © Michael Alexander, 1966, 1977, 1991, 2008. Reprinted by permission of Penguin Books Limited.

MACMILLAN COLLECTOR'S LIBRARY

**Own the world's great works of literature in
one beautiful collectible library**

Designed and curated to appeal to book lovers everywhere,
Macmillan Collector's Library editions are small enough to
travel with you and striking enough to take pride of place
on your bookshelf. These much-loved literary classics
also make the perfect gift.

Beautifully produced with gilt edges, a ribbon marker,
bespoke illustrated cover and real cloth binding, every
Macmillan Collector's Library hardback adheres to the
same high production values.

Discover something new or cherish your favourite
stories with this elegant collection.

**Macmillan Collector's Library:
own, collect, and treasure**

Discover the full range at
macmillancollectorslibrary.com